blunts tales

A COLLECTION OF SHORT STORIES FROM THE WORLD OF DADDY P.I.

E. J. FROST

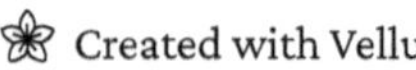 Created with Vellum

author's note

This collection of short stories arises out of a collaborative writing project on Patreon. I joined with a dozen other authors to write short stories in response to a random, weekly prompt. After getting the prompt, I asked my patrons to pick the character(s) who would feature in the story.

I have been amazed not just by how much I enjoyed writing these stories but how invested they have made me in secondary characters in the *Daddy P.I.* series.

I hope this is just the first volume of *Blunts Tales*, with many more to come.

Although this collection is designed to be enjoyed by any reader, readers may wish to read the *Daddy P.I.* series first. In terms of timing, this story takes place after *Missing Ink* and before *Daddy P.I. 3.0*. I have tried very hard to avoid spoilers for *Daddy P.I. 3.0*.

The stories in this collection contain strong elements of power exchange. For a full listing of content warnings, please see my website, https://emmafrostuk.wordpress.com/warning-here-be-monsters, BEFORE reading the book.

a noisy tail

MASTER ROB AND SHANNIE – SHANNIE

IT'S TUESDAY.

On Tuesdays, I start the day at seven with the Shanleys, where Mrs. has Parkinson's and Mr. is in a wheelchair after a stroke. They have a night nurse, but she leaves before they get up, so I usually have to bathe them as well as clean. Today, Mrs. Shanley has wet herself, so her bed needs changing as well. That's my first job of the day.

At two, I take the crosstown train to Hell's Kitchen for my afternoon job with Mr. O'Hara, who has dementia. He should really be in a home, since he's becoming violent. But his daughter won't agree and she's paying the bills, so I show up four times a week and am careful to clean the other rooms first so I don't agitate Mr. O'Hara. When I have to clean the living room, where he's watching TV, I start by bringing him a can of Coke and a tennis ball. The Coke keeps him distracted for a few minutes while I run the vacuum, which upsets him the most, and the can won't shatter like a bottle. The can doesn't hurt as much as a bottle if he throws it at me, either. But he usually throws whatever else is at hand first, which is why I give him the tennis ball.

At seven-thirty, I'm on another train, headed crosstown again, this time to a swankier zip code. I get off at Lexington and 63rd Street and walk the four blocks to my third job. I'm grateful for my New Balance tenny shoes as I walk, even though they cost more than I could afford when I bought them. Without them, my feet would be aching much worse than they are.

They'll be aching even more after a few hours in the stilettos I wear for my third job.

I enter the club through the staff entrance off the underground car park. This entrance spares the house submissives both the potential scrutiny and the security check at the members' entrance. But it's also a reminder of our place at the club.

I press my thumb to the fingerprint scanner and step into the staff elevator which whisks me silently to the club's second floor. My friend Cappa, who first noticed me in an underground kink club and told me about Blunts, is on the desk. I check in with him to make sure Master Rob hasn't rescheduled our scene, although the Masters here are all about communication and Master Rob would have sent me a text. We part with hugs and cheek kisses—Cappa's such a blessing to have as a friend—and I make my way to the club's changing room.

Normally, I'd be squeezing into the black satin and lace basque uniform of a house submissive, but Master Rob specified a French maid costume for tonight's scene. The outfit, still wrapped in plastic, has already been hung up in my locker, probably by Cappa since he's on desk duty. He's such a love.

After a quick shower to get rid of any smells from my cleaning jobs, I trade my real maid's uniform for a fantasy maid's uniform. It's cute, I have to admit, with soft, white lace edging the bustier and ruffled petticoat. I tie on the lacy wristlets and make sure the garters holding up the fishnet hose are secure before I toddle off down the hall on the five-inch stilettos.

We're doing the scene in the club's huge library. It takes up a whole corner of the block-long building, going up three floors with a wrap-around mezzanine in the middle. It looks how I thought the public library would look when I came to New York from North Carolina, with towering shelves of leather-bound books and brass step ladders on wheels. The lighting's soft, from a huge, central chandelier and reading lamps with green-glass shades placed on small tables. I weave between seating groups of wing-back leather chairs to a spiral staircase up to the mezzanine where we're doing the scene.

Although I'm five minutes early, the Master is already there. Masters can wear anything they want, and some of the crazier characters wear leathers and fetish gear. Not Master Rob. He's dressed nicely for our scene, in a silver-gray, button-down shirt that sets off his dark hair and deep tan. His black slacks are pressed with a crease. I try not to listen to club gossip, but if I did, I'd believe the rumor that Master Rob comes from money.

He acknowledges me with a nod while he unpacks a leather case.

"Good evening, Shannie. Please kneel there with your head down and your hands behind your back."

With a little pop from my tired knees, I kneel where he's indicated in the middle of a circular, Oriental rug and cross my wrists at the small of my back. Like everything at Blunts, the rug's beautiful, done in rich reds, blues, and oranges. I follow the pattern with my eyes while I wait for Master Rob.

Of the many blessings I've received since leaving Earl, North Carolina, Blunts is the biggest. It's elegance and serenity in this noisy, dirty, confusing city. It's safety and peace, far away from judgment. It's the family I always wanted, instead of the family I was born into. I'm thankful for Blunts every day.

But some days, like today, when every bone is separately aching, when the odors of the day are still clogging my nose even after my shower, it's hard for me to enjoy the blessing as much as I should.

Master Rob finishes arranging things on a table and walks

around behind me. He rests his hands lightly on my shoulders, his thumbs stroking the back of my neck.

"Give me three words that describe how you're feeling, Shannie."

Tired. Sore. Smelly.

But that's not what he wants to hear.

"Excited. Tingly. Nervous."

He digs his thumbs into my neck and upper shoulders and I feel a little of the day's weight fall away.

"Try again, sweetheart. Three words that describe how you're feeling."

The Masters aren't mind-readers. I know that. But sometimes I think they have built-in lie detectors.

"I'm sorry, Master Rob. I'm tired, sore, and smelly, but I didn't think you'd want to hear any of that."

He chuckles softly. "I understand, but I'd always rather have honesty. Would you like to know why?"

I would, actually. I kind of get why the Doms here insist on honesty. It's important that they know if we've reached a physical or emotional limit during a scene. But the honesty they demand about *every*thing seems over-the-top.

"Yes, please, sir."

"I'd planned certain things for the scene which might be too strenuous if you're already tired and sore. Knowing that you are, I can adjust the scene to be more comfortable for you. We'll both enjoy it more if you're not distracted by how tired and sore and smelly you feel. Do you understand?"

That does make perfect sense, and I feel the fool for not just being truthful up front. "Oh, yes, sir."

"I'm going to start by giving you a massage to get your blood flowing and ease some of those sore muscles. While I'm doing that, you're going to drink some water, which will flush the toxins out of your muscles and help you feel more alert. I don't smell anything offensive on you, but I have scented massage oil which might make you feel more fragrant. Would you like lavender or shea butter?"

"Shea butter. Thank you, Master Rob, but shouldn't I be giving you the massage?"

"Mmm, maybe another time."

He hasn't given me any idea of what scene we're going to do, other than he wanted me in the French maid uniform and that we wouldn't be having P-in-V sex. Which is fine by me. I don't listen to club gossip, but it would be hard for me not to hear the things some of the other Masters say about Rob. That he's a "soft" Dom. And by "soft," they really mean "weak." But until about a month ago, when they seemed to part ways, Rob regularly scened with DirtyGurl, one of the club's serious masochists. So the whispers didn't make much sense to me.

That left me feeling off-kilter coming into this scene. Nervous wasn't a complete lie. Nor was excited, because Masters rarely specifically request me for scenes. I was excited when the request popped up in my club inbox. Now, I'm more confused than ever. I should definitely be the one giving him a massage. If this was Master Ten or Master Franco or even Master Martyn, I'd be kneeling in front of him rubbing his gnarly feet by now.

That I'm not is certainly a blessing, but I'm not sure what to make of it.

He moves away for a moment and returns with two bottles. Cracking the top on one, he holds it to my mouth and gives me a long drink of the cool contents. He sets the water by my thigh, pops the top on the other bottle, spreads a little on his hands, and tucks it away before kneeling behind me and running his slick palms from my wrists up my arms to the costume's cap sleeves. The warm, nutty sweetness of shea butter rises into my nose. It's so much nicer than disinfectant, or what the disinfectant smell covers. He smooths the oil into my skin, then starts working his fingers down my biceps, kneading, rolling, pressing all the tightness out of my muscles.

I try to keep my position: knees together, back straight, like I've been taught, but his touch is heavenly. I sag, my shoulders dropping, my knees spreading on the plush carpet.

He massages all the way down to my wrists, then works on my hands, pushing his thumbs deep into the pads of my palms. Relief radiates up my arms, spreads through my chest. He pulls on each of my fingers, stroking and rubbing, drawing every ounce of tension out of me.

"Sir, that feels so good."

He leans in and kisses the back of my head. "It feels good to me, too. Your skin's like velvet. Your muscles are softening under my touch. It's gratifying to feel you respond. We'll work up to more intense sensations later in the scene, but I like to start low-key and build."

I like it, too. I've only been a house submissive at Blunts for nine months, after finishing the three-month training. I'm not a masochist, so I'm not in as much demand as subs like Briar, Fleur, and DirtyGurl. I've done maybe three dozen scenes. But all of them have started at a higher level of intensity.

I really like Master Rob's style.

He moves his hands up to my neck and shoulders. Cupping my nape, he holds the bottle of water for me while I take another long drink, then he guides my head forward, until my chin touches my chest. He holds my head there for a minute, then guides my head all the way back, until I'm looking up at the ceiling. My upper back pops and I sigh with the lovely, loose sensation that spreads down my back.

Master Rob spends several minutes rotating my head, until my neck and shoulders are as quivery as Jello, before he takes my hand and helps me to my feet. He hands me the bottle of water.

"Finish that, please."

While I drink the rest of the water, he arranges a feather duster, a polishing cloth, and three knick knacks on a table in front of me. When I finish the water, he takes the bottle and hands me the feather duster.

"Put one hand on the edge of the table here." He guides my hand to where he wants it. "Bend over until you can reach the whole tabletop with the feather duster."

I do, feeling the stretch in my lower back and calves. The position shifts my weight onto the balls of my toes, which immediately announce their unhappiness. But discomfort is part of the job sometimes, so I hold position.

Master Rob kneels behind me. He runs his hand down my calf, circles my ankle with his fingers, and lifts my foot. The ball of my other foot screams with all my weight on it, but I hold position.

"You are beautifully trained, Shannie. I know this can't be comfortable. I won't ask you to hold it for long." He slips my stiletto off and guides my foot back to the floor.

I shift until my weight is distributed and smile at the praise. No other Master has told me I'm "beautifully trained".

His warm hands stroke down my other leg, lift my foot, and ease my stiletto off. He lines up my stilettos near a wingback chair instead of leaving them a mess. He's nice and tidy, Master Rob. I appreciate that in a person.

The position is so much more comfortable with both feet flat on the floor. I sigh and stretch my lower back.

Master Rob hums and runs his hands all the way up from my ankles to my upper thighs, exposed by the short, ruffled skirt.

"Lovely, Shannie. Perfect position."

My cheeks heat and I'm glad he's not looking at my face, because I know I'm wearing a goofy grin.

"You have beautiful legs," he says, continuing to stroke them. Tingles run all the way up to settle between my thighs. "Do you appreciate these beautiful legs, sweetheart?"

I probably don't as much as I should. My legs are strong from all the lifting and carrying I do in a day. I'm on the shorter end of the house subs. The dancers like Zuki, Fleur, and DirtyGurl tower over me. But my legs are long, which is a blessing, because they look good in the fishnets that are part of this outfit and my normal house sub uniform. Hearing Master Rob admire them warms me all the way through.

"Thank you, sir."

"Please answer my question, Shannie."

"Oh, sorry, sir. Yes, I appreciate my legs. Maybe not as much as I should, but I do appreciate that they're long and strong."

"That's a start. Flex up onto your toes for me, please."

I do, feeling all my muscles tighten. He brings me back down to my heels and tells me to keep my feet flat through the rest of the scene.

His commands—and they are commands, even when they're phrased as requests—are so easy to follow. Nothing like the stress of following the orders of sadists like Master Ten or Master Shedo. They both like to grab me for unscheduled scenes. My nervousness and anxiety do it for them. I understand that's their kink and I'm here to fulfill the Masters' kinks as well as my own, but sometimes it's hard.

Everything with Master Rob is easy.

Especially as he lavishes praise, soft touches, and little kisses over the backs of my legs. My kitty's puddling. He can probably see the wet patch growing on the small, satin panties that are part of the uniform, since I'm bent over the table and the skirt of this uniform doesn't even cover the tops of the fishnets even when I'm standing upright.

He proves he's aware of that growing patch of wetness a moment later when he pushes his face flush with the backs of my thighs and lays a kiss right on top of it.

Only my hand on the edge of the table keeps me upright. Goodness, that's a kiss.

"Thank you, sir," I say shakily.

His chuckle is low and pleased. He kisses the backs of both my thighs. "How's the dusting coming, sweetheart?"

I can't rightly say I've done any dusting since he bent me over the table. I swipe the feather duster over the far edge of the table, hoping it'll make my behind flex and wiggle for him.

I guess it does, because he claps one of his warm, slick palms to one cheek. I bite my lip at the small sting.

"Naughty maid," he says, sounding anything but unhappy about it.

My posterior sure does have a mind of its own. It sways and waves, attracting more of those hot, smarting smacks. They never deepen into pain. He knows just how to hit. Each spank fires through me like an electric shock. Just enough to make my eyes go wide with the impact, then go hooded and heavy at the rush of tingly heat that follows.

He rubs his hands over my warm, round cheeks. "You're doing a very good job there, my sweet little maid."

I'm not really working, at least, not at cleaning, since everything in Blunts is dustless and polished to a genteel sheen. Even so, of all the jobs I've done today, of all the people I've served, he's the first one who's complimented me.

The thrill of his praise warms me even more than the spanking.

"Thank you kindly, sir."

He laughs softly. "I love how your accent peeks out when you get into the flow of the scene, Shannie. You shouldn't hide it. It's charming."

I try to tone down my accent, because my boss at the cleaning service told me on my very first day that it makes me sound like a dumb hick. Something you don't ever want to be pegged as in New York. So I tighten up my vowels, twist any gentle drawl into the harsher, more nasal way that New Yorkers speak.

It's nice to let my hair down and be myself.

"Does your pussy have a sweet, Southern accent too?" he asks.

I giggle and twist my head to look at him. He's standing close behind me, his hands lingering on my curves. He normally has a slightly detached air about him. A lot of the Masters do. Like they're thinking more important things than the rest of us. Not now, though. He's intent, sure, but all the hard angles of cheek and jaw are relaxed. His deep blue eyes are full of light and laughter.

"Sure does, sir."

He laughs, deeper and even warmer. One of his hands steals between my legs. He shifts the gusset of my panties aside and strokes my kitty. He doesn't plunge his fingers inside the way some of the harsher Masters do to watch me jump and hear me squeal. He strokes and draws a low, sweet moan out of me.

"Mmm, that's what I like to hear," he says. "I think I might be able to get your pussy to say just about anything."

The notion has me giggling as he moves away to the other table and retrieves a long, black bullet. He clicks it on with a gentle buzz. I expect him to shove it right in, but he doesn't. He rubs the velvety tip over the backs of my thighs, tracing patterns that have my behind acting up again. I wiggle and wriggle and shift at the tickly, tingly buzz.

He works the bullet closer and closer to my center, finally rubbing it up and down my cleft. I stretch across the table to swipe at the very far edge, pretending like I'm not just about collapsing from the shivery pleasure.

"Is that a good spot?" he asks as the bullet circles closer and closer to my clit. "Your pussy can tell me the truth."

I'm giggling and gasping as I confirm, "Such a nice spot, sir."

"Mmm. How about here?" He rubs the bullet up and down my opening, which has my eyes rolling back into my head.

"Yes, sir."

"I think your pussy would say it with more enthusiasm."

My body's heaving with giggles and pleasure as I say with the enthusiasm of a Marine, "Sir, yes, sir!"

He chuckles. "Very good. You follow direction beautifully, Shannie."

"Thank you, sir." I don't need any prompting to show my enthusiasm. I haven't done anything like this before. It's just purely fun.

I usually struggle a bit to let go and relax during scenes. It's not even an effort to let go as Master Rob works the bullet back and forth from my clenching opening to my throbbing clit. He guides me up, up, up. His hand settles in the small of my back, pushing my belly down onto the table, which makes the ripples spreading up from the bullet so much more intense. My kitty's reduced to helpless moans of delight—which might have a hint of a drawl—as he lifts me up and over the edge into that moment when everything inside me explodes into white light and flashes of hot sweetness.

"Oh, oh, oh, sir, thank you so much!"

He eases the bullet back a bit but doesn't turn it off, letting its buzz coax me gently back down to Earth. It's a lovely ride down, relaxing slowly back into my body. I feel a stretch in my legs, but no ache. Even my feet are comfortable for once, my toes digging into the soft, plush rug.

He finally turns off the bullet with a click. He tucks my panties back into place and moves around me while I loll over the table. I couldn't move if he told me to, but since he hasn't given me any direction, I don't need to.

He gives me time to recover.

When he returns to my side, he takes the feather duster out of my limp fingers. Then he helps me up and guides me over to one of the big wingbacks. He sits and smooths his trousers. There's a soft flush across his high cheeks. The excitement in his bright eyes has faded to a gleam. Every muscle is relaxed as he pats his thigh.

I take a seat in his lap. He wraps a comfortable arm around me, not pressing me to his chest or crushing me.

It's nice. He's nice. Blunts isn't a place I associate with niceness. It's a place of extremes. But in this black and white world, Master Rob is a soothing touch of gray.

"I enjoyed our scene very much, Shannie. Did you, sweetheart?"

"So much, sir." He's not pressing the bulge in his pants into me, but I'm aware of it against my hip. "Can't I do anything for you, sir?"

He hums deep in his chest. "Next time. This was different for me and very, very gratifying. I'd like to keep exploring this with you, if you'd be happy with that. Would Tuesdays and Thursdays work for you?"

He wants to scene with me every Tuesday and Thursday? Something regular like he used to have with DirtyGurl?

"I'd love that, sir."

He picks up my hand and kisses my knuckles. "It's a date. I look forward to hearing that sweet, southern twang from your pussy every Tuesday and Thursday."

I giggle. "My kitty doesn't really talk, you know, sir."

He kisses me on the cheek. "Are you sure about that? It had a lot to say to me tonight."

"It did?"

"Mmm-hmm. All of it good, Shannie. All of it good, my good girl."

a thorny tail

MASTER TEN AND BRIAR ROSE – TEN

OPERATION: *Punishment Scene*

Location: Blunts

Time: 21:30

I'm on time.

She's not.

It should be the first and only time Briar Rose is ever late to scene with me, but it's far from it. She's habitually late for scenes. Her lateness is part of her testing me. She wants me to prove my mastery.

She won't be disappointed tonight.

I check my watch, even though I'm perfectly aware of the seconds that have passed.

21:31:01.

Officially late.

I move from where I've been setting up the punishment frame and take my phone out of my bag. With a tap, I call the reception desk. Austin, a house submissive who would never dream of being less than five minutes early to a scene and who, I admit, bores me, answers.

"How may I serve you, Master Ten?"

"If Briar's pulling her usual shit, she's loitering somewhere around the desk. Tell her to haul her ass in here."

Austin clears his throat. "Yes, sir, I'll tell her."

As expected. She's probably leaning against his desk, gossiping, with that light in her eyes she gets when she's deliberately thwarting a Dom. Although Briar doesn't get along with most of the house submissives, I notice none of them dodge her when she has her "I have tea to spill" face on.

And there's been a lot of tea to spill lately.

I rub my hand over my own face, wiping away frustration and irritation, and return to my preparations.

The last time I used this punishment frame, a very different submissive was strapped into it. If I'm honest with myself—and I'm always honest with myself—I'd prefer it was her I was waiting for. Not that she ever made me wait. DirtyGurl wasn't as eager as Austin, but she was always punctual. She had her own testing moments, sure. All subs do. But she was respectful of my time.

I'm not sure Briar Rose knows the meaning of the word "respect."

She might just learn tonight.

The door to the dungeon—which is not in the basement and is furnished like a harem room with loungers, a huge round bed, and blue drapery everywhere—opens and Briar Rose glides in.

She's undeniably beautiful. Big blue eyes, a mane of red curls, tight body. She wears the house submissive uniform of black satin and lace corset, panties, suspenders, fishnets, and five-inch black-patent stilettos like she was born to it.

But the contents don't match the wrappings. Inside, Briar looks like one of those Jackson Pollock paintings. She's the most emotionally messy person I've ever met. And she likes to splatter all that mess all over everyone around her.

I don't meet her eyes or acknowledge her beyond pointing at the floor near the punishment frame.

She's done enough scenes with me that she knows I want her to kneel there and wait for me. I don't actually need to do any further preparation; I'm ready to start the scene. I've changed my mind about what we're doing and where we'll be doing it. But having a bottom kneel for a few minutes without their top's attention puts them in a submissive headspace. Which is where I like to start scenes.

DirtyGurl would already be on her knees, back straight, shoulders squared, hands behind her back, the way I've taught her.

But Briar's in full brat mode tonight. Instead of kneeling where I've indicated, she perches on the edge of the circular bed. "Master Ten, before we get started, I wondered if we could talk about something."

The obvious answer is no. She knows what I want and she's stalling to test me.

But on the one-percent chance that she has something relevant to say before I start the scene, I humor her. "Yes?"

"You've heard that DirtyGurl's left the club, right?"

The way she asks, it's not a question. Exactly how aware I am of DirtyGurl's resignation was probably the subject of Briar's gossip session with Austin.

Perfectly aware.

Excruciatingly aware.

"And?"

"Well, everyone knows you used to scene with her regularly. I was just thinking . . ."

She trails off. I know what she's fishing for. She wants me to fill in the blank by asking her to take DirtyGurl's place on my rota. I wouldn't have had any objection to Briar substituting in—so long as she was volunteering for weekly punishment—if she hadn't gone about it this way. But part of her messiness is the attempted manipulation of her tops. Although a few of the softer Doms humor her, I think it's a mistake.

"Yes, what were you thinking?"

A pretty pink flush rises to her cheeks. One of the things I like best about Briar is her very pale, very markable skin.

"I was thinking you might want someone to scene with regularly," she says, her voice dropping to just above a whisper.

"Someone, like you?"

It finally penetrates that I'm not rising to her bait. She clasps her hands together before sliding off the edge of the bed and kneeling where I indicated.

"You don't like me presuming," she says, lowering her head and crossing her wrists behind her back. A hint of her twang shades her words. She suppresses her accent usually, which is unfortunate because I like it. If she drops into subspace, it becomes as thick and sweet as molasses. But in anything but subspace, that sweetness indicates that she's stressed.

She's realized she's seriously miscalculated.

I pick up a cane and walk around her, tapping her shoulders until they're perfectly square. She's crossed her wrists left over right, when she knows I prefer right over left. That gets her a sharper tap across the wrists. She gulps as she rearranges her hands. The last part of her posture that I correct is her knees, which are too close together. The cane's cut on her inner thighs makes her gasp and hastily move into the right position.

"I'm sorry, Master Ten," she says.

I believe she is sorry, but it's for absolutely the wrong reason. She's sorry because she thinks she's annoyed me by suggesting I'd want to scene with her regularly. That's not what I find annoying.

"You're sorry because you're late and wasted my time?" I ask with a flick of the cane against the soft skin of her thigh that's not quite a cut but is a lot harder than a tap. "You're sorry because you sat on the bed instead of kneeling as I commanded? You're sorry because you made deliberate mistakes in assuming the position? What, exactly, are you sorry for?"

She closes her eyes. "All of those things."

"Mmm, I don't believe you, Briar. I think you're bratting for attention, which you know I hate. I think you're trying to provoke me, which you should know by now you don't need to do to get a punishment. Try again, why are you sorry?"

She swallows, her pale throat pulsing. "I'm sorry for being tardy. I'm sorry for bein' a brat."

"I doubt it. But you will be. Get up. You're going to the changing room."

Her eyes fly open and she lifts those huge, deep azure eyes to mine. A crystal drop spills from one and runs down her cheek. A crocodile tear.

"You're kickin' me out?"

"No, I'm sending you to get dressed in street clothes. We're going to relocate this scene. Do you have a toothbrush in your locker?"

She nods.

"Good. Get changed into street clothes and bring your toothbrush. You have five minutes to meet me at the reception desk."

"Yes, Master Ten."

She climbs to her feet unsteadily. She pauses, twisting her fingers together anxiously. When I lift my eyebrows at her, she flees, the door to the dungeon slamming behind her.

Much better.

I shed the chest harness I was wearing for the scene and pull a fresh shirt out of my play bag. My leathers and boots are unremarkable in this part of New York at this time of night, so I leave them on. I take a piece of rubber that DirtyGurl gave me as a gag gift and I've never remembered to toss out of the bag and ball it in my fist. The dungeon's reserved until midnight and I might want to use the bed after teaching Briar a lesson, so I leave my bag and stroll out to the reception desk.

Austin's still on duty. As soon as I approach the desk, he bows. "How may I serve you, Master Ten?"

"Keep everyone out of the Blue Harem room. I might want to use it when we get back."

"Of course, sir. Is there anything else I can do for you?"

I shake my head. "I'm taking Briar out of the club for an hour or so but then we'll be back. Is she scheduled for anything else tonight?"

None of the submissives I usually scene with schedule anything afterwards. They know better by now. But if another Master asked for her, Briar might have made an exception.

"No, sir."

I nod and ignore him. He fidgets for a minute before going back to typing at the keyboard recessed into the reception desk.

Briar's back with a minute to spare. She wore heels, jeans, and a long-sleeved blouse patterned with green and gold to the club tonight. The jeans are tight and white. The blouse looks like silk. She's going to regret her clothing choices after this scene.

I sweep my eyes up and down her, then tip my head at Austin. "Transfer two hundred from my account to Briar's. That should cover the clothes."

Her eyes, downcast, flick up to mine, then drop back to the carpet. "My shoes," she whispers.

I guess the heels are designer. "You can take them off."

I like the added drop of humiliation she'll feel, doing the scene barefoot.

"Put your hair back up," I tell Briar. She'd had in the ponytail I require all my subs to wear during scenes but had some kind of lapse of reason in the changing room and took it down so it's a coppery froth around her shoulders.

"Sorry, sir," she whispers as she quickly fixes it back up. She does something with her fingers after securing the ponytail so wisps of hair frame her cheeks.

I will make her so sorry for that little vanity.

"Toothbrush."

She hands it to me and I tuck it into my back pocket. Then I shake out the piece of rubber I'm holding and hold it out to her. "Put that on."

She stares at it in horror.

It's a half-mask, covering the top of the head and face down the cheeks, with holes for the eyes and ears. Tufts of red hair stick out around the ears. The rubber's white with blue diamonds framing the eyes and a soft, red ball for a nose. DirtyGurl gave it to me after I teased her about not being afraid of me—when all the other house submissives rightfully are—and she told me the only thing that truly scares her are clowns.

Because coulrophobia is a real thing, and because I never wanted to truly frighten my DirtyGurl until she tried to leave me, I never wore the mask.

If Briar's afraid of clowns, she hasn't checked it off on her club limits sheet, where DirtyGurl actually did. I think the horror twisting Briar's features is because I've asked her to cover her pretty face and glossy locks with such an ugly thing. She clearly hasn't focused on the fact we're going to be doing a kinky scene in public and she might want a little anonymity.

Another thing I'd miss about DirtyGurl—if I missed her—she's sharper than any tack. One of the smarter women I know, despite her spotty education and criminal history. She'd have realized the purpose of the mask and enjoyed the irony of me having her wear it, in the space of time that Briar's been staring at me, open-mouthed.

"Do you understand my command, submissive?" I ask.

Her fingers shake as she reaches for it. She fumbles it on and leaves it askew, so her long, false lashes catch in the right eyehole.

I take pity on her when I see a real tear slide out from under the mask. I tweak it straight and nod at her. "Out the front."

She teeters on her heels as she turns and walks toward the door to the huge, front staircase.

I prowl after her, enjoying the smooth working of my muscles.

I'm not in the same shape I was in the service. I don't need to be to do what I do now and a leaner physique is both easier to maintain and less conspicuous in the civilian world. So I've been focusing on distance running and free climbing rather than weight training for the last few years and like the changes the different exercises are making in my body.

I hear DirtyGurl's new master is a runner. I'd offer to run with him if he wasn't the enemy.

Out on the street, Briar pauses and waits for my direction. A few pedestrians walking by see the clown mask and snigger. Briar shrinks in on herself, her shoulders curling. I wish I could tap her with my cane and remind her to correct her posture and carry herself the way a house submissive should. Blunts isn't an underground club filled with wannabe twenty-somethings sport fucking, or some weekend munch. The club members are invested in the lifestyle. We hire and train the best. For all that Briar is a pain in the ass some-times, she's earned her basque. She should carry herself like she has something to be proud of.

"Stand up straight," I growl at her. "Remember who you are and who you're with."

Her shoulders snap back. "Yes, sir."

"Turn left and walk down the street to the Penny Drop," I tell her, naming a bar two blocks away. It's the nearest thing to a dive bar in this part of the City and having been in the bathroom a time or two on a Saturday night, I know it'll be none-too-clean. I also know the bartender well enough to walk through with a woman in a clown mask and not get tossed out.

She turns and walks, her heels clicking on the pavement. I assume she can walk a few blocks in those things. They're not as high as the club stilettos and she manages on them all night. I'll keep an eye on her, though, to make sure she doesn't get blisters.

The clown mask barely draws a second glance inside the Penny Drop, which tells you everything you'd need to know about the clien-tele. I wave two fingers at Bert, the vet behind the bar before guiding

Briar to the back. There are three bathroom doors next to the fire exit.

It's tempting to take Briar into the men's room and let her suffer her punishment under the eye of anyone who comes in to take a piss. But I'm careful not to involve vanillas in scenes. They can't give consent and they often misunderstand what they're seeing. Instead, I steer Briar to the door marked male/female which is likely to be a single stall.

It is and from the yeasty acidity in the air as we walk in, neither Bert nor his staff have been through to clean it tonight.

I lock the door behind us and lean against it.

"Take your shoes off and get on your knees."

"Ma-master Ten," she objects, looking around. It rained earlier and the tile floor bears a number of muddy footprints as well as a few scraps of toilet paper that missed their mark.

"Do you understand my command, submissive?"

She shudders but slips off her heels and sets them by the door before folding down onto her knees. She tries to preserve her jeans by settling gingerly onto her knees and toes and resting her ass on her heels.

Since I don't have my cane, I unzip my leathers, take out my cock, and slap her across the face with it.

The move's so unexpected, she nearly falls over and breaks position to catch herself. "Sir!"

"Get in position, girl. Being in a strange place is no excuse for half-assing your way through a scene."

"Sorry, sir!" she wails as she rearranges herself. There are no deliberate mistakes this time and she stops trying to protect her clothes. That's better. The only thing that matters in a scene is submitting. Obeying. Letting everything go and bending her will to mine. She shouldn't be thinking about her clothes or her hair or anything but pleasing her master.

"Good girl." I give her the drop of praise she needs. "Open your mouth."

When she does, I spit into it to reinforce who she belongs to for this scene. Then I feed her the tip of my cock.

"Suck."

For all her shortcomings as a sub, Briar gives magnificent head. She knows exactly what I like, lots of tongue and firm suction at the back of her mouth. I let her suck me until my eyes are rolling back in my head. Then I stop her with a tap on the cheek.

When she releases me, I slap her with my wet cock again, but it's an approving slap this time and she just smiles, even as I paint a line of her own saliva down her chin.

Before she thinks her punishment's over, I tuck my dick away, take the toothbrush she gave me out of my pocket and hand it to her.

"Clean the base of the toilet."

She shakes her head.

"Do you understand my command, submissive?"

Her shoulders draw up and she glances over at the can. "Yes, sir, but I'm not doing it."

I cup her chin. "Look at me when I'm talking to you. Because?"

"It's disgusting and unhygienic and I won't do it," she grinds out.

"I agree it's disgusting. There's nothing unhygienic about it unless you use your toothbrush afterwards, which I would not recommend. As for refusing to do it, you're not leaving here until it's done, so I'd get started if I were you."

Her chin trembles in my hand. The crocodile tears start again, drizzling in black lines under the mask to drip off her jaw.

"No, sir."

"You can tell me no all night, submissive, but unless you're using your safe word, you're doing it. You're inconveniencing anyone who wants to use this bathroom and you're annoying me by delaying. Get to it."

I can tell when the tears change from fake to real by the way her eyes redden. "Please don't make me. It's horrible. I don't want to touch it."

"I'm sure you don't," I tell her. I flick the cleft in her chin with my thumb. "Is submission about doing what you want?"

"No, sir, but no one else would make me do something so gross! I'm not doing it." Her eyes dart right and left. "I want to leave. I want to go back to the club."

"Look at me, submissive. You're here because you chose to submit to me tonight. That means you take what I give you, and what I'm giving you tonight is punishment."

"Then belt me or something! Choke me with your cock! But you can't ask me to clean a toilet with my toothbrush. This isn't a punishment. It's-I don't know what it is, but it's something else. It's gross and humiliating and sick—"

"There are people who would say being hit with a belt or choked with a cock is gross, humiliating, and sick. What matters isn't the action, submissive, it's the mindset. Whether you're taking pain or cleaning a public toilet, the issue isn't whether you're enjoying the activity, it's that you're submitting to me. Do you want to submit to me?"

She nods. "You know I do, sir."

"Then the nature of the activity I've commanded you to perform isn't material. Crawl to the toilet and clean the base. Now."

She cries for a good minute, her eyes searching mine from within the mask's blue diamonds, hoping I'll bend, change my mind, pick a punishment she'd secretly enjoy.

I don't. I've given her a command and I'll wait here until the bar closes if that's what it takes for her to obey me.

Finally, hiccupping on her tears, she nods. I release her chin and follow her as she crawls over to the toilet.

It's not visibly filthy, but it's not something either of us would touch by choice. I lean over to the sink, squirt a little soap from the dispenser into my palm and then run water into my cupped hand. I drop the handful on the floor near Briar's knee.

"Scrub," I tell her.

Still crying, she does.

I stand over her as she works. Does it make me hard to see her on her knees, rubbing little circles of soap along the line of grout between toilet and tile? Does listening to her whimpers and hitching breaths run that familiar electricity through my blood?

Yes, it does. Because, as I told her, this isn't about the activity. It's about submission. It's about me commanding and her obeying. We pretty it up at Blunts. We paint it in shades of pleasure and gild it in costumes and role-play. But this is the heart of submission, raw and maybe ugly to someone on the outside looking in, but beautiful to me. This is what brings structure to the chaos of the world. This is what gets me through each day. This is what battles back the demons when they get too loud.

When she's scrubbed all around the base, I pull off some toilet paper, since the bathroom has one of those noisy dryers instead of hand wipes and drop it by her knee. "Wipe up the soap, put the tissue in the toilet, and throw your brush out. Unless you want to keep it as a reminder."

She shakes her head, the red tufts of hair flopping.

"When you've thrown the brush out, you may rise and wash your hands."

Sniffling, she follows each command carefully and in order. I time her as she washes her hands, making her rub for a full sixty seconds, until I'm sure the antibacterial soap will have killed the germs she's sure to have picked up between crawling and scrubbing.

Once her hands are dried, I stand her in front of me and take her chin in my hand again. "If I do you the honor of asking for another scene, will you be late?"

"No, Master Ten," she says around a sniffle.

"Will you brat to get attention?"

"No, Master Ten."

"Will you enter into the scene with the true desire to submit to me as your master?"

"Yes, Master Ten."

"Will you carry yourself as a house submissive should and ignore the opinions of anyone but your master?"

"Yes, Master Ten."

"Good girl. If you will do all that, then I will see you tomorrow at nine. If you can keep doing all of that, I will see you every Thursday at nine. I won't always give you pleasure, but I will always top you the way you need. Do you understand me, submissive?"

"I do, sir. May I kiss your hand, sir?"

"You may." I open my hand so she can slide her face down and plant a soft kiss in my palm.

"Thank you, sir," she murmurs into my hand.

"Take off the mask, wash your face, and fix your hair. You'll walk out of here with your shoulders back, your spine straight, your head high. You're a submissive of Blunts." I tap the leather collar mostly hidden by the neckline of her blouse. "Honor your collar."

"Yes, sir. I'm sorry for everything, sir."

I believe she is. For now. If I could look inside her, peel back the mascara-streaked cheeks and the once-white jeans that are now brown from knee to ankle, she'd be a Seurat. All those dots of color neatly ordered into a beautiful whole, orderly and peaceful.

But she won't stay that way. She'll be a Pollock again in a few days. Because Briar's truth is that she doesn't want to change. She enjoys being messy and inflicting her mess on everyone around her. It's one of the reasons I've never considered offering her my collar, despite her beauty and oral skills.

I don't expect scening with her weekly to last long. She'll do something to truly piss me off, or she'll get a better offer from another Dom who is more willing to put up with her shit. But for now, it works for both of us. It gives her a certain status among the house submissives. With the club's former queen bee banished to New Jersey and DirtyGurl gone, Briar might even claim the top spot. There's not much that would gratify her more.

For me, it goes a little way toward filling a void I can barely even acknowledge.

a messy tail

MASTER MAC AND DIRTYGURL – BRENNA

I'M DRAGGING ASS.

It has been a day.

It started before dawn, with Mac tossing and turning because today's the day his daughter's being released from the in-patient facility where she's been detoxing from a methamphetamine overdose. I check the time on my phone. He should be finished moving her into my old apartment by now, so maybe we'll both get a better night's sleep tonight. But we both have a lot on our minds, so that might be a vain hope.

I worked a shift and a half at my shop. My arms are aching from holding the tattoo gun for twelve hours. But we're busier than busy, as my grandmother would have said, and down a tattooist until Mac finishes the permitting process for the daycare he's setting up so he can take care of my second tattooist's kid. He ran into a snag yesterday about his CPR certification, so that may have him tossing and turning tonight. He's pushing not just because I'm working so many hours with Fareena out, but also because he's trying to have everything ready for when Logan's daughter, Olivia, arrives.

We're all trying to get ready for that.

Which is why I'm doing the grocery shopping at nine o'clock at night after a long-ass day.

Usually, Emily and I put in an order online on Sunday afternoons, which is when we get organized for the week ahead. But I worked through Sunday, and with Emily out of her head with baby-arrangements, she forgot. I only realized how severe the situation was when I got home and tried to make a coffee to perk myself up before Mac got back. Only to discover we were out of beans and milk.

I grab an economy pack of toilet paper and toss it into my cart.

My phone pings; I pull it back out to check it. Between the baby and Mac's daughter and shit going down at Blunts, there are too many people who might need my attention urgently for me to ignore a notification.

It's a text from Mac.

My Sir: Sure you don't want the coconut oil kind? That brand looks a little rough for sore, subby asses.

I whirl around to find my Dom and fiancée, who must be watching me if he can see the brand of toilet paper I just picked.

His blue, blue eyes sparkle at me from where he's leaning against a display of wine bottles. "Hey, girl."

"Sir!"

He steps away from the wine bottles and holds his arms out. I jump into them. Just the sight of him energizes me.

He gives me a kiss that's wholly inappropriate for the supermarket, or any public place. I revel in it, pressing my breasts against his hard chest and sucking on his tongue when he slips it lazily between my lips. He tastes of black licorice, his daughter's favorite. They've been candy-bonding again.

With a flick at my tongue stud, he lets me up for air. "Good surprise?"

He knows I don't always like surprises. Because the surprises in my life before him were usually of the incarceration or hospitalization variety. But he's been rewiring my thinking with little weekly surprises. Always good ones.

"The best, Sir. I didn't think you'd be back for hours."

"Naomi's unpacked and on a video-call with her tutor. No reason for me to force more one-on-one time with her old man on her."

I shake my head at him, grinning. His daughter adores him as much as he adores her. They've been through some shit, but since she went into rehab, their relationship has been getting stronger and stronger.

He strokes a finger under my chin. "She says thank you for the walls. She loves the murals."

I duck my head. Compliments still make me uncomfortable.

But my Sir doesn't let me get away with that. He tickles me under the chin until I meet his bright blue gaze again. "That was a nice thing you did, girl. Naomi and I both appreciate it."

I smile into his eyes even as my cheeks burn. "You're welcome, Sir."

Naomi's not the only person I've known who has struggled with drug addiction; I've heard more than one story about how crazy-making institutional white walls can be. So I thought I'd give Naomi something pretty to look at. Doing murals of forests and flowers was also good practice for the book I'm illustrating for Emily.

"Mm, I'll show you my gratitude more tangibly when we get home." He strokes his thumb under my eye. "Is it a massage and Rule Seven kinda night? Or would you be up for a scene?"

"Whatever you want, Sir."

Before he showed up, I'd have been begging for a massage night. But now that he's here—and the happiness I always feel when I'm in my Sir's arms is rioting through my veins—I'm up for whatever he wants to do.

"Let's finish this shopping and see how you're feeling."

"Yes, Sir."

I thumb my phone over the shopping list I made. He reads over it, tugging absently on one of my dreadlocks. He never tries to run his hands through my dreads—which is ridiculously painful—but he often tugs on them. Just enough for me to feel the pinch in my scalp, and the flare of heat that follows.

"Alrighty, girl. I'll go get the meat. That's definitely my department. You finish up here and get the oat milk Emmy's poisoning us all with. I'll meet you in the veggie section. Few things I want that aren't on the list."

I snigger at the meat and oat milk remarks and stretch up on my toes for another kiss before I continue through the household aisle. Mac lopes off and returns with easily a hundred pounds of chicken and fish. With Emily watching Logan's cholesterol, we don't eat much red meat as a household, but the two men sure do put away the protein.

I've finished the households aisle when Mac returns with wine and beer. Logan gets some fancy British beers delivered to the house, but Mac knows my pedestrian tastes and loads up the cart with Corona.

He vanishes while I'm hitting the dairy aisle. I find him in produce with a bottle of tomato juice under one arm, comparing bunches of organic celery.

"Bloody Marys, Sir?"

"I have a hankering, girl. We got hot sauce?"

"Actually, that's on the list. Red, green, or both?"

"Both. We can do a little comparison test."

"Red sauce versus green sauce in Bloody Marys?"

"Red sauce versus green sauce on your sensitive parts, girl."

Said sensitive parts clench, and flush with heat.

"Done that, Sir." He tortured my nipples for a slow eternity with hot sauce one day.

"Mm, not the same sensitive parts I'm thinking of."

Said sensitive parts retreat an inch into my body. "Sir, I won't be able to sit down."

"You got oat milk, right?"

"Yes, Sir."

"Best thing for cooling a fiery behind, sweetheart."

I gulp. I've had an overheated ass plenty of times and never put oat milk on it.

"If you say so, Sir."

He nods. "I do say so, girl."

He tosses leafy greens, citrus, and a packet of Jalapeno peppers into the cart. I eye them warily.

"Those aren't going in my behind, are they?"

"Night's young, girl."

"Sir?"

Mac chuckles. "I love that look of anxiety. You know how long we've been together?"

I nod. I've kept track, too. "Two months today, Sir."

"That's right. And I can still get that adorable look of anxiety outta you with just a few words." He tips my face up and kisses the tip of my nose. "Hope I can still get it outta you fifty years from now, my little goddess."

A hot shiver shoots straight down my spine. "I love you, Sir," I whisper.

"Love you, too, Bren."

There was a time he wouldn't say those words to me. Now, he says them every day and I'm never in any doubt that he means them with all his heart.

He puts his arm around my shoulders as we search for the condiments and add the two types of hot sauce to the cart.

***

Back at the townhouse—which I have to start thinking of as our townhouse instead of Logan's, since Mac and I are living here full time now—Mac helps me unpack and put the groceries away. For someone with as much authority and responsibility as Mac has, he never shirks when something needs doing. No matter how menial the task, Mac's right in there, pitching in.

There are a lot of things I love about my Sir. His willingness to do anything that needs doing is right at the top of the list. I've submitted to too many Doms who finish a scene with a kiss and a hug or a bar of chocolate and then take off, leaving the clean-up to someone else. Usually me.

Mac shoo-es me away from a small pile of groceries that he leaves on the kitchen island. I spy the celery, bottles of hot sauce, a lemon, and the tomato juice in the pile.

"While I get ready, fetch me two towels. One to wrap your hair in and one to lie on."

"Yes, Sir."

He clears his throat. "What do I get first?"

I grin and stretch over the island for a kiss. He never lets me leave the room without one, now.

Because both Mac and Logan like impromptu scenes as much as planned ones, there are caches of scene essentials all over the house. I hit the one in the bathroom for towels, a tie to secure the towel around my dreads, wipes, and, perhaps the most essential thing when scening with Mac: lube. My Sir really loves his anal. I put up my hair and wrap it in the towel and tie, since Mac knows I don't like other people messing with my dreads. Carrying my little haul, I return to the kitchen and kneel by the island while I wait for Mac.

Every Dom has their own preferences for the kneeling position and after two months with Mac, I'm accustomed to his. My body settles into position naturally, comfortably. My shoulders back, stomach in, knees wide, hands on my thighs but palms up. I'm naked already, since Mac loves Logan's "no clothes in the house for submissives" rule and enforces it even when Logan's not around. Any discomfort I might have felt about being naked around other people, particularly people I'm not intimate with, got trained out of me as a house submissive at Blunts. But nothing about my time there, not the training or regular scenes, helped me drop so readily into the perfect mindset for a scene. I submit to Mac twenty-four-seven, but nothing makes me feel my submission more than kneeling for him.

Mac makes an appreciative humming noise in his chest as he moves around me. He's down to a T-shirt and worn jeans because Logan keeps the house so warm. The black shirt clings to his biceps and pecs. The jeans cup his ass just right and show off his lean, runner's thighs. Mac's in better shape than a lot of men half his age and watching him, the muscles shifting under his clothes with each fluid movement, makes me drool.

He snaps off a stick of celery and runs the leafy tip down my nose. "I'm going to get you messy, girl."

"I guessed, Sir, since you asked me to put my hair up. I'm good with that."

"Would you do it even if you were unhappy about getting messy?"

Dom question. I smile to myself. "You know I would, Sir."

Mac chuckles. "I love your submission, girl. Means everything to me. Take a sip."

He holds a cup to my lips and I pull in a mouthful of rich, spiced tomato juice.

"Roll it around in your mouth. Enjoy the flavors."

I do. Mac knows I like tomato everything and even though the drink would be that little bit better with vodka, it's still delicious.

He has me sip until I finish the cup. Mac always makes sure I'm hydrated going into a scene. That caring, which goes far beyond our scenes and is unlike anything I've had from my previous Doms, is also high on the list of things I love about my Sir.

"Good girl. Onto your hands and knees. Stretch out your hip if you need to. Then crawl over to the dining table."

"Yes, Sir." I'm used to kneeling so my bad hip isn't too tight. I wiggle side to side just to keep it loose, before I crawl across the cool floor to the table. Like a lot of the furniture in Logan's house—our house—it's a big, old, heavy piece. Solid wood. It's held me, and

Emily, plenty of times and I don't have any doubt I'm going to end up on it now.

Mac gathers up the towel and lube I've brought and follows me. When I reach the table, he flicks two fingers so I return to a kneeling position. He spreads the towel on the table, then offers me his hand and helps me up onto the towel.

He arranges me on my back, with my arms over my head, wrists crossed, my feet on the edge of the table, knees wide. He can see everything, touch everything. The vulnerability would bother me, but I trust my Sir absolutely. If he wants to see me, I'm his to gaze at. If he wants to touch me, I'm his to stroke, prod, pinch, strike.

He leans over me, running his fingertips from my wrists, down my arms, along my ribs, rounding my hips, up and down my legs. I grin up at the ceiling when his touch trickles over ticklish spots. He doesn't linger. He's not trying to tickle me. This is just a gentle warm up.

Once my skin's tingling, Mac disappears for a moment and returns with a tray that he sets down next to me on the table. He takes a cup and pours a little cool liquid into my belly button. I have to suck in a breath to keep from giggling. Mac grins at me before lowering his head and sipping up the tomato juice. He finishes by tugging on my belly piercing with his teeth.

"Ow, Sir," I whine, even though it doesn't hurt.

I had a recurring infection there, because my favorite leather pants caught the piercing wrong. But between the little nurse I now live with and Mac taking my pants to the tailor to be altered when he took his dress shirts to the drycleaner, it's so fully healed I don't even feel a twinge.

He tugs harder before his mouth drifts south. He licks across my bare mons before rimming my spread lips with the tip of his tongue. It takes every ounce of control I have to keep my hips on the table.

"Oh, Sir."

"Mmm. Delicious, girl. Let's add a little spice, huh?"

Thinking of Mac "kicking it up a notch" down there makes me

giggle. Mac laughs when I share that thought. My laughter ends with a gasp when Mac traces the same path with a burning fingertip.

"Oh, Sir!"

"Sting, girl?"

"And burns, Sir."

"Good, tell me if it itches."

It doesn't itch, but it makes me wriggle all the same as my most delicate skin sizzles. My thighs tremble and Mac runs his palms up and down them, holding me open wide as he dips his head again and licks the burn up and over my clit.

My back arches up off the table. "Sir!"

"Mmm, it's going down next, girl."

I grit my teeth against the spreading burn. It will morph into needy heat, I know from experience. But the initial burn is excruciating.

Even as my eyes prickle, my core tightens. A bready musk perfumes the air and Mac leans over me again to take a deep sniff.

"Getting turned on there, girl?"

It's not really a question. Mac knows exactly what he does to me. He slides a finger into me, immediately finding the evidence of my arousal. He pumps his finger in and out leisurely.

Never stopping the slow, deep stimulation, he tips a bottle over my opening. A few cold drops slide down my cleft. My ass-cheeks clench at the temperature; I force myself to relax and take what my Sir is giving me.

It's a gentler burn this time. Probably the green hot sauce, which never packs the same punch as the red one, at least not to my tongue. Or my ass. It's a mellow warmth as Mac works it in with his thumb, but it's the motion of his finger inside me that keeps me arching, not the burn in my ass.

Mac puts down the bottle and picks up the celery stick. He tickles my nipples with the leafy end for a minute before reversing his grasp on it and thwacking my clit with the broad end.

Although it makes an impressive sound, there's barely any sting. Just a nice thump that reverberates through my belly.

Mac holds up the celery stick, which bends at a right angle. I snigger.

He shakes his head in disgust. "Clit, one. Celery, zero."

I giggle. "I can't help it if your stick isn't up to the job, Sir."

Mac chuckles. "Careful, girl. Plenty of sturdier sticks I could use."

I scoff. I can't help it, even though I'm not a brat and rarely try to provoke Mac, but it's just such an easy target.

Mac thwaps my clit with three celery sticks. Still barely any sting but there's a solid thump that makes me gasp and squirm.

He withdraws his finger, which makes me whimper with loss, switches hands, and uses the three celery sticks to start up a steady thump-thump-thump rhythm that shoots bright sparks up into my belly with every hit.

Another warming trickle down my cleft is followed by several squirts of something colder and more slippery. Knowing, and very happily anticipating, what's coming next, I push my feet wider on the edge of the table.

"Here we go, girl. How much d'you think this is gonna sting?"

"It's not too bad, Sir," I promise.

He doesn't look reassured, his brow beetling as he looks down between our bodies. The celery's rhythm never falters as his thick head pushes between my now-slick cheeks. The sensation is so familiar, even with the unusual warmth from the hot sauce, that I just relax into the spiraling pleasure from the pressure of his head on my sphincter and the steady drumming on my clit.

He hisses and more cool liquid slides over where we're joining. "Girl, you know I think the world of you, but I've never admired your pain threshold more than this moment."

I laugh. "I've always known I could take more heat than you, Sir."

He strokes in and out, his frown smoothing as the lube spreads and pleasure outweighs whatever burn he's feeling.

"Better, Sir?"

"Mmm. Not a fan of that first bite, girl."

"You have to push past that, Sir."

"I see that." His strokes become more fluid. My body tightens, my muscles locking, as he pushes wave after wave of sensation through me. His hand flattens on my belly, intensifying the ripples from the percussion on my clit. "Stay with me, girl."

That means he wants us to climax together. It's something he's started asking me for in scenes. There's a mental discipline to it, matching my pace to his, when I usually chase my orgasm as soon as I feel it start to build. It keeps me focused on him, watching his micro-expressions, the way his jaw tightens, the flush that spreads up his throat and tints the edges of his ears. His eyes darken as his thrusts gain an urgency, a pounding beat, that I follow.

It lifts us up together. There's a moment where we strain: him into me, me around him. Our bodies lock together. The tension rises to a fine, shimmering point. Then it breaks over both of us, me convulsing around him, him convulsing into me. Heat that's both alike and unlike the burn of the hot sauce floods me. His deep groan ripples the air a moment before my gasps of release.

He slumps over me. I tip my head forward until our noses touch. We breathe together for long, quiet moments.

I feel closer to Mac than any person I've ever known, and never closer than these moments, where I feel all our boundaries dissolve and our hearts draw as close as our bodies.

"I love you, my Sir."

"I love you, my girl." He shifts to hold himself up on one forearm. I think the discovery that he's still holding three sticks of celery is a surprise. He tosses them onto the table with a grunt and a lazy smile. "Should we make Lo and Emmy a late-night snack with that celery?"

I laugh. "Hot celery pudding?"

Mac snorts. "Although you're always delicious, girl, I can't see that being a hit."

He eases out and wipes me so carefully he doesn't even spread the lingering burn.

"Thank you, Sir."

He takes my ankle and starts rubbing upwards. He works all the way to my hip before switching legs and rubbing upwards again. My toes are tingling by the time he's finished and my legs are steady when he helps me off the table. I press up and kiss his cheek to thank him for the aftercare.

"You're welcome, girl. Into the kitchen. You start on the rice and I'll start on the beans."

I tip my head. "Beans and rice, Sir?"

"I'm betting you didn't eat because you were working and I know I didn't eat because I was helping Naomi get settled, and neither of us needs to go to bed on an empty stomach when we've got a house full of food. So we're going to make Bebe J's black beans and rice and wash it down with a beer or two while we watch the late news."

I salute him. "Aye-aye, Sir."

He grabs the celery and smacks me across the ass with it, which sends me running into the kitchen, giggling and wiggling my ass at him.

My Sir, brandishing a handful of broken celery stalks, and laughing his good, deep laugh, follows.

*a waggy tail —
part 1*

CHAIRMAN CHESS AND TESSA – CHESS

BARKING and yipping penetrates the sanctuary of my office.

I rub my fingers over my brow. My skin feels both tacky and greasy from working through the night. Since my computer is now cycling as the dividends are paid out to the club's members, I take the moment to reach into my desk drawer and pull out a Fulton and Roark towelette.

There was a time, not even a year ago, that Sara Ann would have been kneeling by my chair, patiently waiting for me to finish. She wouldn't have let her master work all night, and if I'd insisted, she'd have been the one to wipe my brow.

She took good care of her husband and master.

I don't look at the empty space next to my chair as I wipe my face.

While the computer's still processing, I stand and walk over to the window. My office is on the penthouse level of the club and has a commanding view down into the central courtyard.

The flapping of a temporary awning stretching off the club's Stables catches my eye.

I grind my teeth. That's not fastened properly. It could hit someone. It could expose what's going on in the tent to the ever-curious eyes of our neighbors or air traffic, of which there's a lot in the City.

With a last check of my computer to make sure the payments have gone through, I toss the towelette into the stainless steel can next to my desk and storm downstairs.

The sounds that were a distant din up in my office are a cacophony when I walk out of the Stable door into the courtyard. But the sounds are nothing to the utter mayhem taking place under the flapping canvas. Puppies running in circles. Puppies dragging their trainers by their leashes. Puppies splashing water over everything out of bowls they should be drinking out of. When Pence runs up to me and lifts his leg like he's going to relieve himself on my Armani suit, I bellow, "What is going on here?"

Silence falls over the tent.

Austin, the house submissive who is nominally in charge of organizing this madhouse, rushes over to me, clutching his clipboard to his chest. "Master Chess, how may I serve you?"

I point at the awning.

Austin follows my gesture. "I'll have that taken care of immediately, sir."

"See that you do."

I start to turn on my heel when another house submissive runs up to me and kneels at my feet, holding a leash in her mouth. Although I'm less than impressed by this event, I have to admit she looks lovely in a black lace teddy, suspenders, and fishnet stockings. Spotted ears attached to a headband holding her straight, sleek hair back from her face, "paw" gloves on her hands, and a fluffy "tail" detract not at all from her beauty.

"Hello, Tessa," I say.

She gives a soft yip around the leather loop in her mouth.

"Master Chess," Austin says hesitantly, "Master Martin's been delayed so Tessa doesn't have a trainer. Is there any chance . . . would you have a few minutes to spare? We're just training for the puppy trials and Tessa can't do the course without a trainer."

I glance from Austin's pleading face to Tessa, who tucks her gloved "paws" to her chest and blinks her big, brown eyes at me.

"Tessa, I—"

"Please, Master Chess?" Austin pleads. "Tessa's worked hard on this. It's not her fault Master Martin's delayed."

My excuses wing away on the breeze generated by the flapping canvas. I wave at it. "Get that fixed. Tessa, show me what you've learned."

She yips sweetly. I take the leash handle from her mouth and follow her as she drops to her hands and knees and crawls toward the center of the tent.

In an area marked off by a ring of safety mats, there's an obstacle course set up. My eyes drift over a ramp that our new ponyboy, Allyn, is scrambling rather clumsily over. The star of our nightclub, Fleur, is weaving through a set of upright posts on her hands and knees, probably bruising her perfect skin. She's yapping at the top of her lungs at Javier, one of the club's sternest sadists, who slaps her ass to spur her through the course so playfully it can barely be called a slap. Justine, her magnificent mane of gray-white hair streaming, jumps for a soft rubber ring thrown by the usually unsmiling Mistress Dana. Dana grins and claps as Justine catches the ring in her mouth.

I let Logan hold one role-play night and this is what happens. The submissives we've invested countless hours training crawl around scraping their hands and banging their knees. The masters who spend years perfecting their aim with flogger and whip are reduced to throwing rubber rings.

Tessa turns and kneels at my feet, pulling her "paws" to her chest again. She looks up at me.

I cup her face. She doesn't deserve my foul mood. Austin said she'd worked hard to master the course. She's never been anything other than a hard worker. She went through her training to be a house submissive in record time. She works five nights a week in the nightclub without complaint, never asking to move up into the more prestigious and better paid positions inside the club. I only hear praises from her Doms.

She deserves better from me.

"Have you enjoyed the training, darling?"

She nods eagerly and yips.

"That's a good girl. Where does the course start?"

She turns and crawls toward the ramp. I follow, holding her leash carefully so it doesn't pull at the spiked collar enclosing her throat or trail on the ground. She waits at the base of the ramp until Allyn's clear. Felix, our Master of Festivals, sweeps Allyn up in his arms, tickling the submissive under his chin while calling him "a good boy."

Once the hurdle is clear, Tessa gamely scrambles up. At the top, she balances, holding up first one "paw" and then the other, before she crawls down the far side. At the bottom, she poses again, lifting each paw, and throwing me an imploring glance over her shoulder.

I clap. "Very nicely done, darling."

She prances through the upright poles, weaving through them gracefully, wiggling her shapely bottom with its plumed plug. Grudgingly, I admit to myself that this has not been a waste of her time. Training, in whatever form, is good for our submissives.

She stops on a circular mat and poses, both paws up. When I hesitate, she tips her head toward a basket full of rings and balls. I pick up a ring and toss it up in the air for her.

She pushes off with her strong legs, catches the ring, and returns to her pose, paws up. I clap again.

"Very pleasing, Tessa."

She preens, shifting from side to side on her haunches so her tail swishes across the mat.

"Lovely, dear girl. Is that it?"

She shakes her head and tips her head toward Allyn, who is now prancing around the outside of the ring with Felix holding his leash.

"Ah-ha," I say. "Show me your paces, darling."

Tessa tosses her head, spotted ears flapping, and follows Allyn, stopping every few steps to pose, or twirl around on her haunches, or "point," one paw and one leg lifted, showing off her balance.

When she finishes the circuit, she stops beside me and paws my leg. I clap and look around for something to reward her. How can there not be a box of treats handy?

When I snap my fingers, Austin appears again, still clutching the clipboard. "The tent's secure, sir."

I check and when I see the taut canvas, nod my approval. "Well done, boy. Don't we have treats for our good puppies?"

"Uh, most of the trainers have been rewarding their puppies with a grooming session, sir, but I know you won't want to do that and Master Martin's sent me a text saying he's only ten minutes away, so if you want to just end things here, Tessa won't have long to wait for Master Martin."

I look down at Tessa, who is blinking up at me with her big, brown eyes. She's done very well. She's stayed in her role the whole time. She's mastered the obstacle course with grace and skill. She's sweet and pliant. Generous in both giving and receiving pleasure, according to the reports I get every month.

Maybe it's time. If not to fill the empty place beside my chair, then at least to be part of my club again.

I smile down at her and stroke her cheek. "Now, darling, what kind of trainer would I be if I passed my puppy to someone else for her reward? Would you like a reward from me?"

She nods eagerly, brown eyes shining.

"Yes, you do. Let's do the course once more so I can see how perfectly trained you are and then I'll take my lovely puppy up to my office for a good grooming. Would that suit you, darling?"

She clasps her paws together and whines sweetly.

"Perfect girl." I clap Austin on the shoulder with my free hand. "Well done, Austin. Let Martin know I've got it from here. If he doesn't want his prize puppy stolen, then he should be on time."

Austin hides his grin poorly. "Yes, sir, I'll tell him."

I snap my fingers at Tessa, who eagerly trots toward the ramp. I follow a step behind her, keeping the leash taut but not tight. As she scrambles up the ramp and goes into her first pose, the reddish light from the overhead heater gleams over her shoulders and arms, glistening on a light sheen of sweat. I think of how she'll wriggle and moan as I "brush" her with lips and palms and finally, my cock, until her whole hide is glowing.

"That's my very good puppy," I tell her. "I can't wait to give you your reward."

She smiles, and yips in delight.

Continued ...

*a waggy tail —
part 2*

CHAIRMAN CHESS AND TESSA – CHESS

MY PENTHOUSE OFFICE is quiet when I lead Tessa into it.

When I left less than an hour ago, I was frustrated. Sara Ann would have called me "frazzled." I wouldn't ever use that word, certainly not about myself. But I was ready to rip someone a new one.

Returning with Tessa crawling at the end of her leash, I'm calm. Almost . . . happy. It's not just the delight of having a beautiful woman crawling behind me. It's seeing our house submissives training, working hard to please their dominants. This is how the club should be. I shouldn't have disdained what appeared to be chaos. The members and house submissives rely on me to lead them, to see past the surface to the truth of matters.

I saw truth today crawling on its hands and knees. Jumping in the air. Reveling in role-play outsiders would demean, but brought joy to members and house submissives alike.

I glance back at Tessa, who has crawled all the way up from the Stables, not whining or complaining or even breaking role once.

I stop, turn, and kneel in front of her. She immediately sits back on her haunches and raises a paw.

"You're such a good girl. I'm sorry if I started things off on a sour note. You're a delight, Tessa." I run my hand over her soft, shiny hair. "I've already had a very long day but would you like a grooming session and then a late breakfast before I turn in? You can speak to answer me."

She clears her throat, which is probably sticky from all the animal noises. "Thank you, sir. That would be a very big reward. Can I do anything for you? You look so tired, sir."

I smile gently. I am tired. In more ways than one. "Are you free for the rest of the day?"

"Yes, sir."

"Then spend it with me, my good girl. I need a few hours of sleep and then we'll see if we can find a scene or two this afternoon before dinner at the Trattoria. Does that suit you?"

She beams. "Yes, sir."

"Good girl." I straighten and give her leash a gentle tug. "Into my office, sweet puppy, and up on the couch while I get my grooming tools."

She crawls through double-time. Her eagerness causes a warm stirring in my chest. She leaps gracefully onto the office couch and poses there, paw and leg lifted, showing her balance again. I run my hands over her back to praise her.

"You pose beautifully, darling. I can tell you've worked hard on your balance."

She wriggles happily under my hand, her tail swishing across the backs of her legs.

"Get comfortable while I get some things."

She settles onto her side, her legs tucked up, and I give her a pat before I go to find my long-neglected toy bag.

I open it in the bathroom, while I collect towels and the massage lotion. I haven't opened it in over a year. Not since Sara Ann got sick. I'm glad I opened it in the bathroom, away from Tessa, because a whiff of Sara Ann's perfume rises from the bag when I unzip it, and when I look up into the bathroom mirror, that scent-ghost has made my eyes over-bright.

I wipe my eyes on a towel and take out some implements to groom my puppy with. Tessa deserves my full attention, not my lingering grief. I pass over any toys that have Sara Ann's name on them. It's time to box those away with her clothes. A horsehair brush with an unadorned wooden back is perfect for my puppy. As is a little leather paddle with three cut-out hearts. Satan's heart, Sara Ann used to call it. She loved the marks it left. That will give my puppy a nice burn and pretty marks to enjoy later.

I roll the toys into a towel with the lotion and carry them back through into my office.

"Sit up, darling. Beg me nicely for your grooming."

She does immediately. So eager. She sits up on her haunches, back straight, paws curled to her chest, and lets loose a series of imploring whines and yips that go straight to my balls. Delicious.

"Good girl. Show me how to take off your pretty teddy. I don't want to rip it."

She spreads her knees on the couch and paws at the crotch. I reach down and find the snaps, flick them open, and draw the teddy carefully off over her head. It really is a lovely thing. Not at all the usual outfit for our house submissives, but I think I'll add it to the costumes available to them. It's sweet and alluring in a way the uniform basque and G-string aren't.

"When we're done today, you'll tell me where you got this, sweet girl. I think all of our house submissives should have it available as part of their wardrobes. So pretty."

She nods eagerly.

I stroke back down over the path the teddy's traveled. It gave hints of her smooth skin, but seeing everything it concealed is breathtaking. There's something so arousing about a woman's body. All those lush dips and curves. Tessa's shaped differently from Sara Ann, with a narrow upper body and full hips. But every woman's body, no matter what shape, is glorious. Something to be appreciated, worshiped, adored.

I kneel next to the couch.

"Tessa, look at yourself, you darling girl. Look at these beautiful breasts." I weigh each of them in my palm, plucking her brown nipples. She's very tan, but in the lighter triangles where she was covered by a bikini, there's a deep olive cast to her skin that I've never noticed before.

I should have paid more attention.

She looks down at herself and then back at my face. She gives me a soft whine.

With a final squeeze, I release her breasts and run my palms down her sides to her hips. I grip them hard enough to leave fingerprints and watch her pupils expand to swallow the brown of her irises. Oh, yes, she likes a Dom's firm grip.

"Your hips are delicious." I squeeze again and then shape the curves with my palms. "Perfect for my grip. Wonderful girl, will it be too much for our first time if I fuck you from behind and get my fill of these gorgeous hips?"

Panting softly, she shakes her head.

"Good girl. But not yet. First you need a grooming, don't you? Look what I have for my good puppy." I unroll the towel and pick up the brush. Her eyes flick from the brush to the paddle lying on the towel. A soft whine escapes her throat. "Yes, yes, dear girl. You'll get the paddle, too. Be patient."

She whines a little louder and I chuck her under the chin with the hairbrush. She tips her head up, asking for more. I stroke the thick, soft bristles down her throat. Sara Ann preferred straight strokes because she was very ticklish, but Tessa doesn't seem to be, so I try swirling the brush as well as giving her long strokes. Both make her arch and moan softly.

"Lift your arms over your head," I instruct after swirling the brush over her shoulders and biceps. The backs of arms can be exquisitely sensitive and are too often ignored. She obeys gracefully and I take my time making figure-eights with the brush from her elbow to an inch above her armpit, where she might be ticklish. She wriggles and pants, arching her back so her breasts jut toward me.

That's too much temptation. I lean forward and take one brown berry in my mouth and suck while stroking up and down the other breast with the brush.

A moan rises to a choked bark when I nip. Ah, her nipples are sensitive. How delightful. I'll definitely be clamping these nipples at some point today.

I switch breasts and give her other nipple the same laving, sucking, biting attention that has her writhing and gasping. Is there any better sound than a submissive giving herself over to the pain and pleasure her dominant gives her?

I lift my head and praise her while I stroke the brush over her stomach. "Delicious, darling. You are absolutely delicious. I love your little noises. I can't wait to hear them when I'm inside you, filling up my puppy and making her come."

She shivers and a flush rises in her cheeks, spreading down her throat.

"Darling, are you coming already?"

She whines, high and needy. She's close.

"I'm not ready to fuck you yet. You can have the handle of the brush in your sweet cunt if you need something to squeeze on. Would you like that?"

She nods frantically.

"Perfect, perfect girl." I give her what she needs, spreading her with my fingers and rubbing the handle of the brush through her wetness before slowly sliding it into her.

She throws her head back and howls. The head of the brush, embedded between her thighs, jerks with the contractions of her orgasm. I help her along by pinching her clitoris gently and tugging.

She loses position, her arms dropping to her sides as she arches up off the couch, shaking all over with the force of her climax. I wrap my arm around her hips to keep her from falling off the couch. I could ruin her orgasm in punishment for not holding position, but I've never been that kind of Dom. Ten and Karl and their cabal would scoff and call me soft, but there's nothing I enjoy more than seeing my submissive lost in pleasure. Ecstasy should not be wasted.

As she comes down from her peak, she realizes what she's done. Whining, she puts her paws over her face. When I remove the hairbrush, she shuffles around on the couch until she can put her forehead on the cushion, her paws behind her back, abasing herself to me.

I stroke her head. "Sweet girl, that's very good. You know you made a mistake, and I will correct you, but it will only be a correction. Puppies make mistakes, don't they? But you're trying so hard, being so very good, I can't find it in my heart to punish you. I'm so pleased with you, Tessa."

She whines softly and when I slide my hand under her chin and lift her back into a sitting position, she blinks tear-filled eyes at me.

I lean in and kiss her tears away. I don't criticize her for them. Many submissives get emotional during scenes, particularly when their dominant is effusive with praise, as I've been. People get so little positive reinforcement in our day-to-day lives that it can be overwhelming for a submissive to have praise heaped upon them. It's natural both for the submissive to be overwhelmed and for that emotion to manifest as tears.

"Yes, darling. I know. But you're doing so well. Turn around and hold on to the back of the couch while I give your lovely back and legs some attention. I won't be able to resist the siren call of your hips for long, so expect me to fuck you in this position. If for any reason you need me to stop, reach back and slap any part of me you can reach three times. You may also speak to use your safe word. Nod to show me you've understood."

She nods firmly.

"That's my very good girl. Turn around, sweet puppy."

She spins slowly, carefully, watching the placement of her feet so she doesn't kick me accidentally. She has the experienced submissive's awareness of her body that's so pleasing. When she gets in position and bends slightly, lifting her ass, I reward her with long strokes of the hairbrush down her back. That the handle is now sticky in my palm widens my smile. I'll have her lick it later.

When I get down to the base of her spine, I take a minute to appreciate the glory of her haunches. Every woman should be appreciated in this position. The graceful curve of the spine. The round mounds of her buttocks swelling from her indented waist. I balance the brush in the small of her back while I show my appreciation, squeezing and kneading her ass.

She drops her forehead to the back of the couch with a moan.

"Such a beautiful, beautiful behind. Especially with the accent of this tail." I release one of her delectable buttocks to tweak the tail, pulling on it so the plug strains the rim of her sphincter, then releasing it so the silky fur swishes as her ass sucks the plug back in. "Mmm, I want to fuck you with the tail in so I can see it swish as I pound you but I also want to take it out so I can fuck that tight ass. Such a dilemma."

She giggles.

"Yes, enjoy yourself at my expense for the moment, darling. You have a correction coming and I think now's the time to deliver it." I rub my palms firmly over her ass cheeks, warming the skin. Then I pick up the paddle and give her a firm swat down her left cheek.

Her golden-brown skin flushes the most becoming pink. I can't keep from rubbing it, feeling the warmth under my fingers as the blood rushes in. She wriggles wildly under my hands. Enjoying her correction a great deal, which I don't mind at all.

I flip the paddle over and swat her right cheek.

She moans and rubs her thighs together.

"Like that, do you, my naughty puppy?"

Her answering yip is muffled in the couch leather.

"Yes, I know you do. Here's another two and then it's time for my puppy to get fucked."

She arches her back, tipping her ass up. Asking for the paddle, wonderful submissive that she is.

I give her firm, fast swats and rub in the sting, enjoying the faint heart shapes visible in the welts of these harder impacts.

"You have hearts on your ass, darling. I'll refresh them in a few hours and then pose you in the hall so everyone can enjoy them. Such a beautifully marked puppy."

She keens, a long, sweet sound of desire and submission.

I continue rubbing with one hand while I open my trousers. I've always given my cock to my submissives sparingly. They can have my mouth and fingers as they desire, but they have to earn their master's cock.

Tessa has more than earned it today.

I flick her tail out of the way and hold it to one side with my thumb while I rub my cockhead up and down her puffy lips. She's so slick I slip in without even pushing. At her long moan, I play, dipping in, pulling back, teasing her. She whines and wriggles, but I hold her still while I sip from the bitter-sweet cup of denial. My heart thumps in my ears. There's surely no greater rush than having a woman beg for you to take her.

I sink into her on a long, low groan. That unparalleled tight warmth encloses me. I push until my balls meet her skin. Her back flexes as my tip kisses her cervix. She doesn't object, but I don't think that's a sensation she enjoys. I adjust my angle so I'm pushing into her C-spot instead before I unleash the tension coiling in my back and ass.

Tessa howls and throws herself back, impaling herself on my cock, her hips twitching and flexing under my hands.

I can't help but chuckle. "Oh, darling, coming again so soon? Pace yourself, my puppy. You have a whole day of orgasms ahead of you."

She's too far gone to show any restraint, bucking and shuddering as she milks me. I make sure this is a deep, extended orgasm, pumping hard and dragging my corona over her G-spot again and again as she howls and shakes. Her loss of control is as delicious as the tight contractions working my shaft.

"Yes, sweet girl, let it all go. Let me feel you come."

Shaking, she sags against the back of the couch, pushing her half-mask and ears out of position as her cheek mashes into the fabric. I grin at her abandon and take my pleasure, working myself up and over into my release with fast, shallow strokes until the last few when I push deep and pump her full.

I hold her in position through the aftershocks, my cock jerking inside her as I release months of loneliness and grief. She mumbles to herself, soft little sounds that heighten my enjoyment. I stroke my hand down her back before leaning over and kissing the back of her head.

"You are an absolute joy, Tessa. Thank you very much for giving yourself to me."

"You're welcome, sir," she whispers. "Thank you."

"Would you like a bath with me before we have breakfast? I worked through the night and now I've worked up a bit of a sweat. I can shower on my own, of course, but I'd enjoy bathing my puppy."

"I would love that, sir."

"Good." I withdraw from her slowly but don't clean her up as I usually would. I want her to feel my come running hot then cold down her leg. That little mark of mastery. I even like the idea of it dripping onto my couch and leaving a stain I'll see the next time I work late.

Once I'm confident the couch is marked the way I want and Tessa's had a moment to recover, I help her up and kiss her forehead before leading her into the bathroom for the rest of what I anticipate will be the best day I've had in a very, very long time.

a dino tail

MASTER HAROLD AND PENCE – HARRY

"RAWR," says the dinosaur.

Recognizing Pence's voice, I look up. "Rawr?"

He stands in the doorway of the dungeon I've booked for tonight, his slender frame concealed in the bulky, orange folds of a blow-up T-Rex costume.

I chuckle. "Is this your way of saying you want to cosplay, boy?"

"No, Master. I lost a bet. I have to wear this until Friday. Please, sir, can I have permission to take it off for our scene?"

I finish polishing the crop I'd planned to use for tonight's scene and put it back in my toy bag. There's no way I'm letting him duck out on a bet, so it doesn't look like I'll be using it tonight. Unless there's a back flap on that thing.

"How do you relieve yourself, boy?" I ask.

"There's a zipper down the tummy, sir, but if I open the suit, it deflates."

I snigger. "How do you breathe?"

"There's a fan in here, sir."

"A fan? That's just recycling what's in the suit. What happens if you fart?"

My boy laughs. He has a couple of different laughs. I usually hear his sarcastic snicker because that's the way my boy's sense of humor runs. But he also has a soft, sweet laugh that he lets out rarely, when I've managed to catch him off guard and truly tickle his funny bone. This is the latter.

"I have, sir. It's pretty gross."

I zip up my toy bag and walk over to him. There's a clear panel at the neck of the costume through which I can see Pence's handsome, fine-boned face. It's slightly steamed up, which tells me the fan's not quite up to the job. New York's weather, always changeable, has finally turned toward winter, and it's cool in the club today, so it's not the room temperature that's fogged his windshield.

The costume has the dinosaur's signature short arms, bulbous head, and round haunches. There's a long tail that's going to get in the way of my usual enjoyment of my boy. The costume's vinyl looks fairly sturdy, but it certainly couldn't weather our usual impact play.

Pence's eyes follow me as I circle him, inspecting the costume. "Please can I take it off, sir?"

"I don't think so, boy. You lost a bet, fair and square. That means you keep the costume on until Friday." The date niggles in the back of my mind. "Isn't there something on Friday?"

"Yes, sir. It's Master Rob's charity auction. I'm being auctioned off in the costume for kids' parties or whatever."

I rub my finger under my nose to keep from laughing at him again. Pence has a soft, sweet side that I've managed to dig out from under his habitual cynicism, but it doesn't extend to kids. He loathes small humans. Kids' parties in the dino costume will be a form of purgatory for my brat.

I'll have to rig the auction and make sure Ryan or someone with lots of kids wins my boy.

The costume's hands and feet don't look as puffy as the rest of it.

I close my hand over the suit hand and feel Pence's long, slender fingers through cloth.

"Gloves and booties?" I ask.

"Yes, sir."

"Ah-ha, if you can use your hands and feet, then you can service me well enough."

"Sir, please let me take it off? Or at least open the zipper? You won't be able to fuck me—"

I interrupt his rising objections. "No, I won't. Something you should have thought about before you took the bet. Better make sure I enjoy myself tonight, or your ass'll be sorry next week."

I chuckle at the whine that rises from him. I've come to enjoy his whining. Falling for my boy was a slow process. I've known Pence for coming up on a decade. When he joined the club as a house submissive, he was barely out of his teens and the twenty-eight-year gap in our ages felt much too wide for me to even play with him without feeling like I was cradle-robbing.

But Pence has grown up in the time I've known him. He's become a man I enjoy spending time with. He has a lively mind and a cutting tongue. He doesn't always put that tongue to the best use. Most notably, he turned it against Logan's sweet submissive, Emily. He did it to support his friend, but it was inexcusable. Fortunately, Logan took care of it with a punishment scene that's become the stuff of club legend. All I've had to do is reinforce the lesson a few times, which has worked well into our dynamic, since Pence prefers to brat and I've developed a taste for brat-taming.

What started as a casual scene or two became a once-a-week thing, became a twice-a-week thing, became him coming home with me on the weekends, became him giving up his lease and moving into my place in Little Italy. I'm not home every night and I have a place in Maine that I like to retreat to when living in New York gets to be too much for this country boy. Two hours in at my place on Mousam Lake and Pence is whining about mosquitos and the lack of

Starbucks. So I leave him to his Starbucks and his fashion friends while I fish and ride my Harley on the quiet, country roads.

Strangely, our time apart every few weeks makes our time together better. I guess there's something to the "absence makes the heart grow fonder" chestnut.

I wrapped up my latest fishing road-trip yesterday and got back to the city mid-morning. Pence was out at a shoot—possibly wearing the costume, which makes me grin as I inspect him—so this is the first time I've seen him in almost a week.

I've missed the brat.

"Anything you need to tell me before we get started? How's the wrist?"

Pence has a part-time job as a fashion designer. A "textile artist," as he calls it. Whatever. He sews fancy clothes. Or glues them. Or sometimes staples them, which seems like an odd way to put together clothes to me, but the most I know about fashion is that I'll always prefer 501s to 505s because putting a zipper that close to my balls is asking for trouble.

Pence is pretty enough to model the clothes he wears, but he says he prefers life behind the camera. Pence has his own forms of vanity but posing for pictures that'll be Photoshopped out of all recognition ain't among them. He still takes care of himself like a trip down the catwalk is imminent, though.

I make sure to ruin his carefully-styled hair, beard-burn his exfoliated cheeks, and welt his perfectly-tanned skin in every scene. Gives me a real sense of accomplishment.

All of that's gonna be tough with the blow-up costume between him and my toys, but I'm guessing he won't be so pretty and fragrant after a day in that thing.

But before messing him up, I always check in with him. He'd been having trouble with his left wrist after sewing a ridiculous number of sequins onto a dress. I made him see the club doctor before I left last week, because Pence has his flighty moments. He'll spend ten hours a week and half his income getting waxed, massaged and whatever the hell microblading is, but try getting him to spend an hour taking care of something that can't be seen and suddenly he doesn't have a spare minute until next November.

"Much better, sir. Doctor Chang gave me exercises to do and a referral to a specialist if it's not completely better in two weeks."

"Good." I make a mental note to thank Al for taking care of my boy. The club doctor treats members and house submissives alike for scene-related injuries, but he doesn't have to make time for anything else. He almost never turns anyone away, particularly the house submissives, many of whom don't have good health insurance, but I never want him to feel like we're taking advantage of him. "Take off the gloves and booties."

I return to my toy bag for the plastic tube I keep my canes in. If I'd known about the costume beforehand, I'd have planned an electrical play scene. I'd love to see my boy wriggling and writhing in that silly suit while I zap his tootsies. Maybe I'll make him wear it again for that.

The idea of tickling his toes catches hold and I rummage in my bag until I find my case of sensation toys. I set the containers out on a table, open them, and take out my tools.

Pence shuffles over to stand next to me. This close, I can hear the whirr of the fan keeping the suit inflated, which makes me chuckle.

"Can you sit in that thing, boy?"

"Sort of, sir."

"What would be best, a chair or a stool?"

"A chair if I can sit backwards on it so the tail hangs off."

I chuckle and retrieve a straight-backed chair from a corner of the dungeon. "Plant yourself, boy."

Watching Pence settle into the chair, with much huffing, gets me chuckling again. This scene is going to be all sorts of amusing.

Once he's seated, I examine the ankle cuffs of the suit. They're flexible, so I push them up his calves, admiring his lean muscles and smooth skin. Pence has the nicest skin of any submissive I've played with. Given how much he spends on his ridiculously convoluted regiment, he should. But it sure is a pleasure to touch when we scene.

I prop his feet on a low stool and go back to my bag for a bottle of coconut oil, which I prefer for scenes because the smell puts me right back on Ogunquit Beach as a kid. Rubbing a little oil between my palms, I massage it into his calves, working over the prominent bones of his ankles and heels, up his instep, and around his toes. He groans as I work my thumbs into the knots I find. His bare hands, ridiculously incongruous against the striped, orange suit, flop over the chair back. Pence usually has perfect posture, but now he slumps in the chair, the head of the dino suit lolling forward. It's so bulbous, atop the dinosaur's thick neck and non-existent shoulders, it looks like a cockhead.

When I share this observation with Pence, he sniggers. "Dick-asaurus Rex."

"Terrible," I tell him, although his humor secretly amuses me, but we both enjoy it when I play into the stern Dom stereotype. "Close your eyes."

He sighs and slumps even further into the chair. "Yes, sir."

It's good to see him relax into the scene.

I start with a feather out of my sensation kit, brushing the soft tip over the balls of his feet. That draws another groan out of him and his toes curl. I already know Pence isn't particularly ticklish, but I keep the pressure on the firmer side as I brush the feather over each instep and circle his heels with it.

Hearing his low groans, seeing his toes curl and flex, I feel the first lift toward topspace. It's like a mellow adrenaline rush, a gentle surge of intensity.

Knowing how much Pence likes scratchy sensations, I turn the feather around and gently scratch with the quill, following the same path: balls, insteps, heels. Pence's groans gain a breathy edge.

"Enjoying that, boy?"

"So much, sir. I had no idea my feet were so sensitive."

"Mmm, feeling it in your balls?"

"Yes, sir."

"Pull one hand inside that suit and get it on your dick."

He never moves faster than when I let him touch himself. His hand disappears like lightning and the dinosaur's tummy ripples with motion.

I reach into my sensation kit and pull out a pair of vampire gloves. I fit them over my hands and secure the straps across the back of my wrists. The six rows of tacks built into the gloves are not so sharp that they'll break his skin without a good amount of pressure, but together, they deliver a powerful rasp.

With the vampire gloves, I start on the tops of his feet and drag the gloves over his toes before returning to his soles. He moans and wiggles his toes at the sensation. The tacks leave beautiful, red scores on his golden skin.

I work the gloves over his soles in the same order: balls, instep, heels. Following a pattern gives my submissive some peace of mind. In a scene that may be filled with overwhelming sensations, they know what's coming next when I follow a pattern. It also helps keep me on track when it's easy to get lost in our mutual pleasure.

Speaking of which. "Where are you, boy?"

I've given Pence a pleasure scale to use so I can gauge how close he is to orgasm. My boy loves his orgasms. He'll do almost anything for them and denying him orgasms is the harshest punishment I can give him.

"S-six, sir."

"Good boy. Keep it there for me for a few more minutes."

I scratch the soles of his feet until his toes are curling again. Then I switch over to something that will really make his toes curl: a rattan cane.

I start with the thickest cane. It will give him more of a thump than the sharp sting of a thinner, whippier cane.

I line up his feet side-by-side on the stool and hold them still by pinching his big toes between my finger and thumb. Then I warm him up with the big cane, tapping upwards from his heels toward the balls of his feet and back down.

The dino suit ripples with the movement of Pence's hand.

When his soles are an even, dull red, I switch over to a junior cane. Slimmer, whippier, this cane will give Pence a sharp sting, almost a cutting sensation, with each stroke. That should bring my masochistic brat right up to the edge.

I tap the cane against his heels several times to build his anticipation. He's no stranger to the cane, and loves it on his shoulders and ass, but I've never used it on his feet before. I roll my shoulder to make sure I'm warmed up before I lift my arm in a Cavalry Cut swing, my preferred style of caning because it brings the cane down perfectly flat. I only want to hit my target, not overswing and bruise the flesh on the far side of my strike-surface.

I focus on the skin of Pence's feet as I make the first cut. There's barely any ripple as the cane lands—the skin of Pence's feet is too tight over the muscle and sinew beneath to move much—and the skin blanches white before it shades to pink and then to deep red.

Perfect.

Pence gasps. "Oh, God, thank you, Master."

"Good boy. Bring it up to a seven now."

"Yes, sir." The dinosaur's belly ripples and jerks wildly.

I swing the cane again, half an inch above the last cut on his heel. It's another clean, straight cut that blanches then colors. Pence groans and pants, his toes twitching against my fingers. I lay down another stroke on his heel before I say, "Up to an eight now, boy."

"God-yes, God-yes, thank you so much, sir."

"This is going to be on your instep and it's going to hurt like a bitch, boy. Stay with me."

"Yes, sir. I will. I will-oh!"

He gasps as the cane slashes straight across his insteps. His legs shake, the bunched vinyl over his thighs quivering like Jello.

"Master, Master, please!"

"Hurt so good, boy?"

"Yes, sir!"

"That's my boy. Three more. Last one's going to be just at the base of your toes and you'll be feeling it in your bones. Come after the last cut. You have permission."

"Thank you, Master!" The dino-belly shivers and shudders like the ground during an earthquake. "Thank you so much—"

I slash the cane across his insteps as he's still thanking me. A high whine breaks out of him and then a babble of thanks.

"Second to last one. Work it up to a nine for me."

"Yes, sir! I'm there, sir! I'm so close!"

"Good boy. Here it comes." I give him barely a second's warning before I land the cane again, just below the balls of his feet. Every inch of the dino suit is flapping now, the rustling of the vinyl drowning out the whirr of the fan. I can barely hear the whistle and pop of the cane over it.

He never stops pumping, even while he issues a short scream after the cut and then pants as he processes the pain.

"Good boy," I praise him. "Last one. You can come and then I'll rub you down."

"Thank you, Master," he pants. "Thank you. I love you, Master."

I reach out to rub his head and then remember it's under that ridiculous mushroom of vinyl. "I love you, too, boy. Get ready. Last one."

"Yes, sir. Yes, sir—"

I slap the cane across the balls of his feet, right below his toes. I use half the strength of the other cuts because this is an exquisitely sensitive area. Despite the reduced force, Pence screams, then screams again. But I know the sounds of Pence's different screams as well as I know his different laughs. The second scream is orgasmic. It's deeper, from the bottom of his chest as his body contracts. He arches back in the chair, the suit rippling, the thick orange tail lashing across the floor. I can't see his face through the fogged panel, but I've seen him come hundreds of times and I envision his lips peeling back from his teeth, aristocratic nostrils flaring, eyes rolling and his forehead drawing up like a zipper as the pleasure squeezes and squeezes and squeezes him in its bright grasp.

With a last gasp, he folds forward over the chair again. The suit shimmies, this time with his shuddering breaths instead of the movement of his arm. I watch until his breathing steadies. Then I put my tools away, pour out a little more coconut oil, warm it between my palms, and begin rubbing it into the bright red wheals decorating my boy's soles.

"Muh-master, will I be able to walk?"

"A-yuh. I'll follow this with some aloe. Then you can rest for an hour or two and you'll be right as rain."

"Thank you, sir." He's quiet for a moment while I rub. "I didn't mean to say it during the scene, Master."

I know what he didn't mean to say. We agreed he wouldn't tell me he loves me during impact play. But I only agreed to it because he was worrying himself into a lather over it. And he was only sent into a lather because one of the other house subs convinced him that declarations of love during scenes are a form of topping from below. An attempt by a submissive to dominate the dominant.

I don't and never have felt that way. In my experience, there's no time truer, more honest words are spoken.

I'm not particularly worried about Pence topping from below, either. My boy is a submissive through and through. He brats to test boundaries. He acts out to get attention. But as soon as I hold firm, he settles immediately. He only wants to know what every other person on this planet wants to know: that he's safe and loved, and I'll happily show him that in every scene, in every minute, for the rest of our lives.

"I'd rather you say it whenever you feel it, boy, than hold those words back because you think it's the wrong moment. Life's short. If I died tomorrow, would you be sorry you said you love me today?"

"No, Master."

"Then stop worrying about it." I finish with the coconut oil, wipe off my hands, snag the tube of aloe out of my bag, and begin working that into his welts. Pence sighs heavily.

"Feel good, boy?"

"Everything feels good, sir. Except that I'm sitting in a big wet spot."

I chuckle. "That'll teach you not to lose bets. What was the bet over, anyway?"

"It was with DirtyGurl, sir. She's just learning to swim, so I bet her I could hold my breath and swim underwater longer than her. I guess Master Mac's taught her better than I expected."

I chuckle. I understand why Pence made the bet. After the summer debacle, I've encouraged him to patch things up with Emily. Although DirtyGurl's outwardly the most unapproachable of Emily's inner circle, she has a soft heart. Winning her over would be a good first step.

I also understand why Pence lost. DirtyGurl may be an inexperienced swimmer, but she's a very experienced submissive. Although I've never given her a test drive myself, I've seen her in action plenty and she deep throats better than any pro. I bet she can hold her breath for at least a full minute. Her new master is also a former Navy Master Chief. If she's not already, she'll soon be swimming like a fish. The odds were stacked against Pence from the get-go.

"Well, you know what that means," I tell him.

"Uh, no, sir, what does that mean?"

"It's a challenge now, boy. I can't have my subbie shown up by Mac's. We'll have to train you up to hold your breath longer. How long did she hold hers for?"

"Over two minutes, sir."

Damn, she's good. I'm almost envious of Mac for a moment. Then I chuckle. "Lots of breath training in your future, boy."

His groan, both pained and eager, helps me end the scene with a smile.

*a party tail –
part 1*

MASTER SHEDO AND TAMSIN – TAMSIN

I'M SCARED.

Scared breathless. Scared stupid.

I tuck my arms behind my back and twist my hands together so the Masters and Mistresses watching me can't see how badly my hands are shaking. I will my knees to stop knocking. Try to force air into my lungs by breathing in through my nose, out through my mouth to a count of five the way I've been taught.

I don't even make it to three before I'm gasping in another breath.

"Sweet pea, do you need a minute?"

That's Master Franco's cool, deep voice. I can't see him, because I'm blindfolded for the auction, like all the other house submissives when we're put up on the block for sale. But I know most of the Masters and Mistresses voices so well I can pick them out, one from the other, without needing to see their faces.

There are only a few I've done so few scenes with that I don't know their voices. The exclusively gay masters like Charles, Felix, and Pence's new master, Harry. The heavy sadists like Javier, Karl, and Nico, who say I'm too fluffy to handle their dominance. And then there are the mysterious masters who almost never play with anyone, like Chairman Chess since he lost his wife, or Master Shedo who barely speaks.

I'm so afraid of one of them buying me.

"Sweet pea," Master Franco repeats. "Do you need a minute?"

His voice unwinds a little of the terrible tension building inside me. Helps my lungs expand. Master Franco's always nice to me. He's a sadist and I know I can't fulfill his deeper needs the way the house masochists can, but he never belittles me for it. I never feel inadequate after a scene with him the way I do with Master Javier or even, sometimes, Master Ten. Franco always praises me and says he likes our low-key scenes when he wants to unwind. I wish the other sadists were like him. It makes me feel better to hear him, to know he's running the auction, but oh, I wish he was out there in the audience and could buy me instead.

"I'm okay, Master Franco," I force out.

I'm trying to be brave. My friends Rachel and Pence and Briar, they're all so brave. They never let the Masters or Mistresses intimidate them. They never shake so hard their knees feel like water. Rachel tells me to fake it until I make it. So I try. They've been so nice to me since I joined Blunts, being my friends, taking me under their wings, giving me all the inside info on the Masters and Mistresses so I know how to handle them. I don't want to let them down. I don't want to let anyone down.

You won't never amount to nothing. You're worthless. You're lucky I'll have you, 'cause no one else would.

I shove away those horrible, hurtful words. I haven't seen Jimmy in four years. Rachel says I shouldn't let him take up my mental real estate anymore. But he was such a fixture in my life, from high school where we met through the four years we lived together after I graduated, that it's hard to untangle his words from my thoughts.

For a long time, they were the same thing.

Master Franco's cool fingers wrapping around my elbow pull me out of my thoughts, pull me out of the short line of blindfolded subs still waiting to be auctioned. He helps me up the ramp onto the stage. I feel the heat of the spotlights on my bare skin. I'm naked. Not nude. Naked. Stripped bare. The way I've learned to be since coming to Blunts. The Masters and Mistresses want different things from us, but they all demand the same thing: we're bare, and real, and honest when we come into scenes. I try my best to do that and never argue when they ask me to start by baring my skin.

I never want to let them down. Even the ones who make me feel more bad than good, they've all been so kind to me. They've all helped me, more than they know. I've never been happier, prouder in my own skin, braver about asking for what I want, than I have since I started working at Blunts. Some of them may only see the way I have to go to be as strong, as brave as someone like Rachel or Pence or Briar, but few of them know how far I've come.

They don't need to know. That's my shame to bear. All they need to see is how well I'm doing now. So I stand as straight as I can under the hot lights, under the hot stares of the people I can't see but I can hear, breathing, shuffling, a whisper here and there. I focus on my breathing, imagining Master Ten holding my chin, looking down at me with the faintest spark of approval in his dark eyes, as he fills my mouth with his thick cock and tells me to breathe through my nose.

In. One, two, three, four, five. Out.

"That's it, sweet pea," Master Franco says approvingly. His hand strokes up and down my arm before the rap of his gavel makes me shiver. "We'll start the bidding on our lovely Tamsin at five hundred. I see five hundred. Six. Six hundred. Eight. I see your eight. Do I have a thousand? Yes, I see your thousand. Oh, two? Two thousand. I have two thousand. Two thousand two hundred? Yes, I see two thousand two hundred."

The numbers go up and up. My head spins. The sought-after

subs like Zuki and Fleur and DirtyGurl before she left the club, they command thousands at the club auctions. Last year, when Zuki auctioned off her anal cherry, it went for over ten thousand. Crazy. Ten thousand just for that? I gave it away to Master Ten the first time he asked. Guess I sold myself cheap.

Because you'll never be more than a ten-dollar whore.

Jimmy's words are drowned in the rising numbers. Over three thousand now. Take that, Jimmy.

The gavel taps. "Three thousand four hundred going once. Going twice. Sold for three thousand four hundred for the Manhattan Cares Shelter. Well done, sweet pea."

He takes my elbow again and leads me away from the hot lights, down the ramp on the other side of the stage. The carpet of the conference room where the auction is held slides cool and smooth under my bare feet as Master Franco walks me through the crowd. I feel the heat of their bodies as they move aside for us. A few of them murmur.

"Well done, Tammy."

That sounds like Master Martin. He's so nice. He likes sensation play and never ends a scene until I've had at least two orgasms. I wish he'd bought me.

Master Franco guides me to a stop. "To the winner go the spoils," he says, the traditional phrase when a sub is given to the winning bidder.

"Thank you, Franco," says a low, smooth, man's voice.

I don't recognize that voice.

I don't recognize the warm fingers that brush my cheeks as he unties the blindfold and hands it to Franco.

But I do recognize the dark, expressionless eyes that hold mine when I open them.

I gulp. "Master Shedo."

"Good evening, Tamsin," he says. He holds out a thick, stiff posture collar. "Kneel, please."

My legs shake so badly that it's easier to sink to my knees than remain standing. He buckles the collar around my neck, forcing my chin up, my shoulders back. He moves around me as he adjusts the collar, smoothing the strap down my back, taking my wrists one by one and fastening them into the cuffs built into the back strap. As he moves, he cocoons me in the rustle of expensive fabric from the tailored slacks he wears, the smell of shoe polish and his light cologne. It's not a scent I recognize. I've never been this close to Master Shedo before. But it's also not something I've smelled before. It's fresh, like the air after a thunderstorm, but there's also a dark, woody, almost burnt note to it.

The combination makes my head spin.

He moves back around in front of me as Master Franco announces KayCee and starts the bidding where he started for me, at five hundred. Master Shedo's hand curves around my cheek, his thumb caressing the skin just under my eye. I'm glad I moisturized today. And didn't wear any makeup. Rachel always wears a full face at the club and some of the masters like to see it all messed up after a scene.

But my clear, smooth, seasonlessly-tanned skin has always been my best feature. I'm not exotic like Zuki or Justine. I'm not Instaglam gorgeous like Rachel and Pence. I'm not even tough and edgy like DirtyGurl and Fleur. But I have great skin. Everyone says so. And the Masters and Mistresses tell me how much they love the way my skin marks.

I hope that will please Master Shedo, too. Because I don't know any other way to please him. He does gang-bangs with Mackie and Char. I think he's done some scenes with Cappa, but if so, Cappa's never talked about them. At least not to me. Not that he would since he's in tight with Master Logan's new submissive, Emily, who likes to lord her wonderful, perfect relationship with Master Logan over my friend Rachel. Without any goss to go on, I'm in the dark on what Master Shedo likes.

There's a terror in that. But a hint of freedom, too. If I just let him tell me what to do, maybe I can please him that way?

"You're not with me, sweet pea," Shedo says, stroking my cheek again.

"I-I'm sorry, Master Shedo. I was just thinking that I don't know what you like."

His smile's slow. Almost humorless. But a little light leaks into his black eyes.

"I like you kneeling at my feet. I like seeing you tremble. I like the flush on your cheeks. I like that your nipples are erect. Do you enjoy a little fear?"

My first reaction is to shake my head. Of course, I don't like being afraid. No one does. Do they?

But then I think back on the scenes I've had with Master Ten. They've been both the best and the worst scenes I've had at the club. The worst when I've disappointed him and he lets me know it. But also, the best. When I take everything he wants me to take. When he pushes me and I get past the pain, and yes, the fear. When he tells me he's proud of me. Then I feel I've succeeded. Then I feel I've excelled. I've beaten everything that's against me. Those are the best moments.

"I guess so, sir. Not so much being afraid, but when I beat it."

His smile tips up at the edges. I think that's a real smile.

"That's very good, girl. Does Franco call you sweet pea for a reason?"

I nod into his palm. "My perfume, sir."

"Ah." He squats suddenly, eye-to-eye with me, which feels very weird. I'm only five-three so most of the Masters, and a few of the Mistresses, tower over me. Master Shedo's a little over six foot and built like a marathoner, all long, lean muscle in his arms and legs. He's not a tank like Ten or Master Tee, who runs the nightclub and is bigger than any of the bouncers. But his strength is evident in the easy way he moves.

He pushes my frizzy, brown curls back from my face and leans in. Up close, he smells even better and the cold, refined lines of his face warm into something handsome. His skin, a deeper golden brown than mine, is poreless. He must moisturize even more than I do.

I hear him sniff close to my right ear and then close to my left. He rocks back on his heels and smiles at me before he stands again. "Sweet and light. Not at all cloying like your friend Briar Rose. I like your scent very much."

"I-I like yours, too, sir."

His lips part to show strong, white teeth. "Petrichor and oakwood. I have it mixed specially. I'm glad you like it." He pauses while the gavel raps. KayCee's gone for fifteen-hundred, which makes a smile slide across my face before I can hide it. The club discourages competition between the house subs, but of course there is a little. He taps a finger across my lips. "Do you know why KayCee sold for so much less than you?"

Embarrassed that he caught a moment of victory I shouldn't have felt, I shake my head.

"Because she didn't stand up there and tremble like you did, sweet pea. It was delicious, watching you. I've gotten my money's worth even if that's all we do."

A dizzying combination of satisfaction and worry shortens my breath again. I've pleased him. A Master no one knows how to please and I've pleased him just by being scared. That's not all he wants from me, is it? That would be such a let-down.

"D-do you want that to be all we do, sir?"

He traces the bow of my upper lip with his finger. "No, girl. I have you for three days and I intend to make the most of them."

His hand drifts away from my face to the placket of his trousers, where he has buttons instead of a zipper. Even Chairman Chess's clothes aren't that fancy. He undoes the buttons one by one, slow and teasing, so I get peeks of silky black hair and smooth muscle before he lifts his cock out.

He's not fully hard, so he might still be a grower, but he's not long like Master Ten and Master Javier. He won't slam the back of my throat or my cervix. But he is thick. Like Coke-bottle thick. And veiny. And pretty. If cocks can be pretty. I've always thought cocks are nice to look at, but I know from listening to the other house subs that a lot of them think cocks are gross. Especially uncut cocks, like Master Shedo's. But I like his. It's a deeper brown than his skin, rosy-brown at the tip and base, like the color of my nipples, which are standing at attention again just from looking at him.

His hand comes back to my face. His thumb flicks over my tongue, which snuck out to wet my lips without me knowing. He drags his thumb down over my lower lip and gently pulls my jaw down.

"Would you like me in your mouth for the rest of the auction, sweet pea?"

"Yes, sir."

He smiles again, cups himself and lifts that thick rod to my lips. He taps his tip against my lower lip several times and grins when my tongue steals out for a lick. "Do I taste like rain, girl?"

"No, sir." I lick again just to make sure. "Salty and, mmm, kind of green? Like seaweed."

He barks a laugh which causes some of the Masters still standing around and bidding with numbered paddles to glance over at us. I see their surprise out of the corners of my eyes. I've never heard Master Shedo laugh before. Maybe they haven't, either.

"Do you like seaweed?" he asks.

"Yes, sir. Sushi's one of my favorite things."

"Excellent, now I know what to feed you. Lick me until I'm wet, then take me down, girl. I want you to hold me in your mouth and suck on me until the end of the auction. Then we're going to go to the after-party and I'm going to show off my prize. You look very flexible, sweet pea. Are you?"

"Yes, sir. I did cheer in high school." And I've been teaching fitness classes ever since. That's how I financed my escape from Jimmy. That's how I support myself in the big city, although working at Blunts pays good.

"Excellent," he repeats, with a nod.

As soon as he stops speaking, I open my mouth and extend my tongue, the way Master Ten's taught me. Shedo's eyes spark the same way that Ten's do. He shifts forward and pushes his thickness between my lips.

I swirl my tongue around him, getting him wet as he's instructed. But also enjoying the heat and firmness and texture of his cock. He stretches my jaw a little, but otherwise it's comfortable to give him head. He doesn't plunge down my throat the way Ten would. He lets me work at my own pace, drawing him deeper and deeper into my mouth. I wish I had my hands free so I could jack him a little or play with his balls, but I can tell having me collared and cuffed is a turn on for him. And maybe it's easier for both of us. He doesn't have to worry about me touching him in a way he doesn't like; I don't have any choice but to relax and focus on pleasuring him with my mouth. I show him how much I appreciate his thoughtful dominance by sucking him deep, pressing my nose into the silky strands at his base.

He rewards me with a groan that I can just hear over the bidding, and a stroke from his long fingers through my curls. I focus on earning more of those soft sounds, more of those rewarding touches, as the auction continues around us. My jaw starts to ache, so I move him around in my mouth and find that sucking on his tip gets me not just moans and strokes, but the faintest shudder through his strong legs. He never thrusts. Barely moves. He just lets me work to pleasure him.

When the gavel falls on the last sub, Pence in that silly T-Rex costume that DirtyGurl made him wear, who gets sold amid a lot of laughter, Master Shedo cups my chin and shifts back until his cock slides free of my mouth.

"I haven't finished you off yet, sir," I protest wetly, my lips and chin covered with spit. I wish I had a hand free to wipe myself off.

Shedo tucks himself away but doesn't button up so maybe that means I'm going to get a second chance soon. He reaches into his back pocket, takes out a white linen kerchief, and wipes off my chin.

"Thank you, sir."

"You're welcome, sweet pea. And I didn't instruct you to finish me off, only to hold me in your mouth and suck me for the rest of the auction, which you did perfectly. Now let me help you up. Your knees must be a little stiff no matter how flexible you are. Then we're going to enjoy the party for a bit before I reward you for being so obedient."

A warm glow starts in my belly and spreads outward until I'm sure I'm shining brighter than Rachel's illuminating foundation. He said I did something perfectly. The shine of that may never rub off.

He holds me by my elbows and lifts until I get my feet under me. Then he takes a handful of thin chain out of his back pocket. One length gets clipped to the posture collar. The other length hangs between my breasts as he fastens the tiny pinchers on each end to my nipples. A squeak of pain escapes me. These aren't the rubber-tipped grippers Master Martin uses. These have little teeth that bite in. If I had my hands free, I wouldn't be able to keep from grabbing at my burning nipples. Maybe that's another reason he cuffed me.

He holds the chain attached to my collar in one hand and strokes my cheek with the other until I get on top of the pain with deep breaths.

"Very good girl," he says, holding my eyes. "Give me the pain of the clamps on a scale of one to ten where one is no pain and ten is your limit."

"S-seven, sir. Maybe seven and a half." More pain than I enjoy but not so much I need to use my safe word.

"Perfect. I'll push you over the next three days, girl. I want to see those lovely, brown eyes go wide. I want to see you tremble again. But I'll never exceed a ten and your safe word always works. I read over your limits before the auction and I don't foresee any barriers to our play, but if I do something you haven't come across before that's a limit, use the safe word 'yellow' so I know and can change the scene."

He read my limits list before the auction? Did he always intend to buy me? Me? The silent and mysterious Master Shedo planned to buy me so he could have three days with me?

"Yes, sir."

He strokes my cheek and smiles before he leads me out of the auction room and toward the stairs down to the nightclub, where we hold the after-auction party.

Continued ...

MASTER SHEDO AND TAMSIN – SHEDO

BLUNTS' nightclub is one of my favorite places in the world.

I've lived in many places. Amsterdam. Bangkok. Macau. Hong Kong. Lagos. Mombasa. Bogata. Seoul. London. Joberg. Anywhere my family and the other Triads required my specific set of skills. But after discovering New York—or, more precisely—Blunts, I made it my home.

When everything went wrong and the Nine turned on my family, I retreated here. I barely ever leave Blunts and when I do, it's only with a complement of paid muscle.

Because the price still on my head is a hundred times what I paid for the lovely submissive trembling slightly at the end of my leash. And that's for a bastard, half-caste son my family never formally acknowledged. I was only good enough to be their shadow, as my father named me. I haven't heard from my full-blooded sisters and brothers, aunts and uncles, for over three years. But the bounty on their heads was a hundred times mine. I doubt any of them survived.

The House of the Yellow Dragon is dead. I may be the only one with a drop of its ancient blood still running in living veins.

I glance at the pretty woman walking a step behind me. For a moment, I envy her the simplicity of her life. The lack of thousands of years of tradition and duty that my father impressed on me when he claimed me and brought me into the House of the Yellow Dragon.

I shake that thought out of my head. Something living in Blunts for the last three years—spending my days in the company of men and women outside my family for the first time since I was inducted as a Red Pole on my seventeenth birthday—has taught me is that everyone is fighting their own battle.

I have watched this woman. I have seen her shortcomings. She does not believe in herself. Her choice of friends is odious. She is easily swayed by their opinions. But I have also seen that thing I long for the most: a woman who is aroused by the taste of fear. A submissive who craves that delicate dance of unsafe safety from her dominant.

That's why I bought her. That's why I've given up three days of my potentially few remaining if the Triads catch me to explore her. To see if she could be the one to wear my collar through the days I'm allotted by the gods.

When I gave my thirty-six oaths, my father promised me a woman of full blood. None of my mother's Kenyan taint, despite her descent from warriors and kings every bit as strong and noble as those my father's house claimed as their revered ancestors. A princess, he promised me, who would serve me despite my ignoble blood and give me children who would be welcomed as full members of the House of the Yellow Dragon.

Children who would not have to stand in the shadows.

But the shadows have always welcomed me. There is safety in darkness as well as danger. The princess I was promised never materialized. If she had, she'd likely be as dead as any other member of my house. And I've never desired a princess.

I want a slave.

I want a woman who will give herself to my mercy, even when I prove I have none. A woman who will tremble at my feet even as she secretly smiles.

My father promised me a family, a house to belong to after my mother died, a place I would always be welcome.

He lied.

When I walked through the door of Blunts for the first time. When I inhaled the mélange of sweat, sex, and pheromones. When I saw the women and men kneeling to their masters. When I heard their exquisite sounds of pain and pleasure. That was the moment I found my true home.

I smile at Tamsin. I will never think of her as Tammy. She is Tamsin. She is sweet words and receptive skin. She is a softly-scented flower. A heated mouth that pulled the deepest notes of pleasure out of me. What is she beneath all of that?

I have three days to find out.

She smiles back, all thick pink lips and warm brown eyes in a round-featured face that reminds me faintly of my mother's home. Am I attracted to Tamsin because she carries a few of those shared genes? Perhaps. There are other submissives at Blunts who are closer to me on the many-branched tree of humanity. But they lack that essential element. The quiver in her chin as her blown pupils meet mine. The unripe berry hardness of her nipples.

I draw her over to one of the tables set up on the nightclub's floor. This space is usually packed and pulsing with dancers. The cream of New York's kink scene come here five nights a week to celebrate our shared desires. I join them from dusk to dawn most nights. I'm anonymous here and there's safety in anonymity, even beyond what Tee and his bouncers create by carefully vetting who they let in. I'm just another shadow adding my own cadence to our shared tribal heartbeat.

That I can carry a whip as a symbol of my rank as a Master of Blunts, which in my hands is as deadly a weapon as a dao or assegai, adds to my sense of safety.

Will my sweet pea be able to bear my whip? Will she tremble and cry when she feels its kiss? Will she leak uncontrollably from her bī while she suffers its burn?

Over the next three days, we'll find out together.

When she stops beside the table, I slide behind her and tease her firm, brown nipples with my fingers. I put my lips to the sensitive shell buried in her fuzz of brown curls to whisper, "Pick the thing you like the most. The thing you crave above all."

She shivers in my arms. The thing she craves the most is not on the lavishly spread table before us. It's not swirled with buttercream or topped with toasted almonds. It's the dark promise in the voice in her ear. The teasing bite of my fingers against her sensitive skin.

"Chocolate cake, sir," she whispers back.

There is a decadent confection on the table. A wheel of sponge covered with a glaze just less glossy than Tamsin's eyes when she sucked me during the auction.

"Mmm," I murmur in her ear. "Let me slice you a piece."

I take the provided knife and cut a generous wedge, slipping it onto a plate and setting one of the club's delicate, silver forks on the side. I hold the plate in front of Tamsin so the rich smell fills both our nostrils.

Carefully cutting a piece with just enough glaze and filling, I skewer the decadent square onto the fork's tines and hold it to Tamsin's lips. "Open, sweet pea."

She does, her pale tongue flicking against her lower lip as though she just can't wait for the taste. I tip the cake into her mouth and watch as her pupils expand at the taste. Pink blooms on her cheeks.

"Good?"

"Sooo good, sir."

"Excellent. That was for your delightful obedience during the auction. Would you like to earn another bite?"

She raps her chin on the edge of the posture collar, she nods so eagerly.

"I'd like you to pose for me. If you can hold each pose for a count of five, you'll earn another bite of cake."

"I can do that, sir," she promises.

I run my fingertips over the plush pinkness of her lips, brushing away a crumb. "I'm sure you can, but can you do so amid . . . distraction?"

Her lips quiver under my fingers and her tongue darts out, this time for a taste of my skin.

"Yes, sir."

"Have you ever been whipped, sweet pea?"

Her whole body shakes. "I-I-I haven't."

I drink in every delicious tremble.

"Then we'll take this a step at a time. Tonight, you'll just have the sound of my whip. Tomorrow, we'll work up to the sight of it. And perhaps the day after, its touch."

She blinks eyes gone pink-rimmed. "Ye-yes, sir."

"Good girl." I feed her another bite of chocolate cake just to watch the tip of her nose flush. "Now, come with me."

She follows obediently, without once complaining about the posture collar or having her arms bound behind her back. I'm timing and won't keep her restrained for more than an hour. It's bad for her circulation. Although I love tasting her fear and will enjoy giving her pain, I never want to damage my submissive.

I lead her to one of three circles marked with fluorescent yellow tape on the dance floor. Two circles are empty. In the other, Pence dances in his ridiculous dinosaur costume, striped orange vinyl billowing. Tamsin giggles when she sees her friend; I can't help but smile at his plight.

I stop in the middle of the circle and turn my back to the dancing dinosaur. Tamsin faces me, eyes bright with both amusement and trepidation.

I set the chocolate cake at the edge of the circle. Everyone at Blunts knows better than to cross the boundaries of an active scene, and no one would dare steal something I've laid claim to.

There are some advantages to my reputation.

I take my time rolling up the sleeves of the gray dress shirt I've worn, enjoying the way Tamsin's eyes track my motions, fixating on the skin I'm revealing, the play of corded muscle beneath it. She forgets what her friend is doing behind me. She tunes out the members and submissives circulating through the party. Her focus is solely on me.

As it should be.

Once my forearms are on display, I unlatch the custom leather case hanging from my belt and draw out a coil of braided, oiled leather. I made this whip, as I've made every whip I've used on a submissive. I cut the leather, dyed it a deep cherry red, worked and braided it into the two-foot length favored for riding in China, rather than the longer length used for spinning top games and fitness exercises. Ten and Karl like to tease me about my "little whip." But the submissives I use it on never tease. They like the precision of my whip.

I play it out between my fingers, letting it uncoil naturally. Tamsin's wide eyes follow each slither of the leather, each flick of the tasseled end.

"Turn around, girl. Balance on your right foot. Lift your left foot and place the sole against your right knee. Turn out your hip. Your legs should create the number four."

"Golden rooster stands on one leg?" Tamsin asks with a smile before turning and following direction.

"Have you taken kung fu, sweet pea?"

"Not me. My, uh, someone I used to know. He did."

"Someone you liked?"

She shakes her head.

"Then you won't think of him or golden roosters or anything but the crack of my whip and holding the position through five cracks."

"Yes, sir," she says, drawing up her leg and settling into position. I wait a moment. With her hands bound behind her back, she might have trouble maintaining balance.

She doesn't wobble.

I play out my whip and flick it overhand a foot to Tamsin's left. If she flinches and recoils from the crack, she'll shift more firmly onto the leg she's balanced on, rather than onto her lifted left leg, where she might potentially fall over.

The whip's whistle and crack silences the party for a moment. When conversations resume, there's a smattering of applause.

Tamsin doesn't flinch.

I crack the whip on her other side, over each shoulder, and for the last crack, above her head. Her shoulders draw up an inch, then slowly drop.

I coil my whip and walk to her. I soothe and praise her with my palms on her shoulders, down her arms, cupping her breasts and giving her nipples, which are still unripe berries, a tweak. She tips her head back against my shoulder as much as the posture collar allows.

"That was perfectly done, sweet girl," I whisper in her ear. I can't see her face, but if I could, I'm confident I'd see that bloom of delight I saw the last time I praised her. It's more than a praise kink, which many submissives have. Tamsin craves approval with the force of someone who has been crushingly, cruelly denied.

I know the signs intimately.

"Put your leg down and relax for a moment while I get the cake."

Sighing, she does. I fetch the cake and feed it to her, giving her an extra bite to reward her for doing so well. There are two small bites or one large bite left.

I have no doubt she'll earn them.

"Can you do the splits, flexible girl?" I ask.

She nods. "Yes, sir."

"Good girl."

I set the cake aside and spot her as she slides down into a full split. She tips her shoulders once, but otherwise doesn't seem affected by having her arms bound. I'll remember her balance for future scenes.

Once she's down, I move back behind her and play out my whip again. I crack it five times in quick succession, in an arch over her head, shoulder to shoulder. She keeps her back straight, head high. When I help her up, there's a glistening spot on the floor.

A drip from her bī. What a sweet slut.

I reward her with a kiss before I feed her the last two bites of cake. She yields, surrendering her lips, opening to the flick of my tongue. I take a deep taste of chocolate before I fetch the cake and let her finish it off, smiling as I watch her clean the fork with a teasing, kittenish tongue.

If we were in my penthouse, with its scrubbed-clean floors, I'd make her use that tongue to lick up the evidence that she likes the fear I give her.

But the club's dance floor, although clear, will never be clean enough for me to make my submissive lick it. I rub out the spot with my shoe while giving her another kiss to end the scene. Then I lead her out of the circle, giving the scene-space to Rob, who is waiting with Shannie. I noticed she didn't put herself into the auction tonight and wonder if that's because Rob had already reserved her time. If so, I wish them well. Rob's a good friend, a good man, and a good Dom. He mis-stepped with DirtyGurl, but I'm confident he'll learn from his mistakes and do better by Shannie.

I draw Tamsin back over to the buffet and get us drinks: a bottle of water that I tuck under my arm and two flutes of champagne. The water will clear out the rich taste of chocolate so we can both enjoy the fizzy wine.

When I look around for a place to sit, a stumpy, orange, waving arm catches my attention. Chuckling, I steer Tamsin to the booth where Harold and his boy—still in his puffy costume—are sitting.

We exchange greetings while I get Tamsin settled and give her sips of water. She watches my face, barely paying attention to Harold or her friend. I praise her focus by stroking her curls while I talk with Harold about his latest fishing trip. He's invited me to his retreat in Maine. Some day, when I'm sure the Triads have forgotten me and I won't be putting my friend in danger, I'll go with him and sit on his dock, listening to the lap of water and the calls of the loons while we try to catch the "granddaddy catfish" that keeps escaping Harold's lure.

Until then, I listen as the size of the fish he caught gets larger and larger. I wink at Tamsin, who glows softly in the aftermath of the scene and under the force of my attention. When my internal clock reaches an hour, I unbuckle her wrist restraints and massage her arms until no knots remain.

"Stretch, sweet pea," I tell her. "Then I think it's time for us to say goodnight. You've earned a reward."

She lifts her arms over her head, stretching luxuriously. From within his shroud of orange vinyl, Pence grumbles, "Haven't I earned reward too, Master?"

Harold chuckles. "Sure have. Your reward's Ryan's daughter's birthday party next Saturday. Kids'll love seeing you dance in that thing."

As Pence's whine rises, I take Tamsin's elbow and lead her toward the elevator up to my penthouse.

"Am I staying with you tonight, sir?" she asks.

Tonight, tomorrow, and the night after, at the very least. After that, it will depend on what's beneath those soft, brown curls, behind those yearning eyes. But tonight's been more than a promising start.

It's given me hope.

And that's worth more than all my father's empty promises.

a snappy tail

MISTRESS DANA AND AUSTIN – DANA

THIS IS A MISTAKE.

I make a point never to mix my vanilla family and my kink family.

I don't break my rules. It's safest for everyone this way, particularly me.

Today looks like the day this particular rule gets broken.

"D, is everything okay?" Lila asks, popping out one of her earbuds so she can hear my answer.

"Of course, sweetheart. Are you looking forward to this?"

She nods and replaces the earbud. I can faintly hear the brown noise mix she's listening to even with the earbuds in. She's so good, my little sister. She knew today, in an unfamiliar place, with unfamiliar people, doing something outside of her comfort zone, would be stressful, so she brought her coping mechanisms. She's got an anxiety ring on each thumb, her brown noise playlist on the go, and I can see the outline of her mini-abacus in her back pocket in case she needs to count. All those will keep her calm and focused today.

Her mother-in-law-to-be's best efforts notwithstanding.

I have nothing against my sister's prospective mother-in-law, Carole. She just doesn't understand Lila. What I'm sure seems like a "treat" to Carole: a boudoir shoot in the ridiculously expensive wedding lingerie that Carole's bought Lila, is everything that triggers the worst of Lila's anxiety.

Throw in the photographer—a house submissive from my kink club, that neither my sister nor her future mother-in-law know anything about—and this is a shitshow waiting to happen.

The reception area of the photography studio is a mad house. Evidently, they've double-booked. In addition to Carole, there are four women in trench coats gathered around the reception desk while the harried receptionist and Austin, the photographer, try to sort out the double-booking.

Austin shouldn't be here, either. From what I've heard the receptionist explaining to the Flasher Girls, as I've mentally dubbed them, the regular photographer is sick and Austin's stepped in at the last minute as a favor.

I am, of course, aware that Austin's a photographer. I know the "day jobs" of all the house submissives; I memorize them when I memorize their preferences and hard limits from their club questionnaires. Austin's taken pictures of me before, when I've done rope-bondage scenes with one of my favorite playmates, Mally. But other than club shoots, I understood Austin mostly did fashion photography.

I certainly never expected to bump into him in this small SoHo studio.

Carole turns away from the reception desk and flashes a triumphant smile at us, even while lifting the three bags she's carrying with the stacked macaroons logo, from the pricey boutique she dragged us to three hours ago to try on ridiculously priced lace and satin. Yes, I let her talk me into buying a set. It shut her up. No, I'm not having my picture taken in it. This is Lila's day.

The Flasher Girls tromp out of the reception area. They're not smiling but they're not scowling, either, and I gather some kind of compromise was reached, some discount offered. They're discussing going out for cocktails as they leave and I feel slightly sorry for the bartender wherever they land.

"Ladies," Austin says. "So sorry about your wait. If you'll come with me?"

His voice is low and smooth, but impersonal, like he's never seen me naked and fucking my screaming submissive with a strap-on.

He holds open the door out of the reception area and into the back of the studio. Carole sails through. Lila taps the back of my hand with her forefinger: her signal that she wants me to hold her hand. I wrap my fingers around hers—her skin is chilled even though it's a blazingly bright August day outside the studio—and lead her through the door.

The back of the studio is separated into four smaller spaces. One space is a changing area with curtained booths and two chairs in front of a long, lighted mirror. The three other areas are boudoir settings. A bedroom hung with gauzy curtains. A red velvet dressing room that wouldn't be out of place at Blunts. And a space that looks like a woodland, with a mural that wraps around two walls, in abstract golds, greens, and browns that looks like sunlight coming through trees.

I know which setting Lila would want. I also know which one Carole will pick.

I take Lila to one of the chairs and let her get settled. She has several rituals that settle her in a strange space and I let her run through them, shielding her from Carole, who is busy inspecting the red velvet dressing room set.

While Lila and Carole are both distracted, I beckon to Austin. I've never done a scene with him at the club. He's not my usual taste in submissive. I'm happy to play with both men and women, but my taste in men is on the sissy side and Austin is as far from a sissy as I can imagine. He's well over six feet and built like a linebacker. It's not hyperbole to say his muscles have muscles.

But he has a kind face, and as he comes close, his eyes are the deepest brown I've ever seen. Like sinking into hot chocolate. Not mocha. Not cocoa. Hot chocolate. Something rich and warm and deliciously satisfying.

I don't use any of the hand signals house submissives are taught to bring him to me. Hopefully, that will make it clear to Austin that I'm not Dana, Mistress of Protocol and feared dominatrix, right now. I'm Dana Chavez, sister to Lila Chavez, who is getting married in six days and needs to touch the back and the arms and the seat of the chair three times before she sits in it.

"Hi," I say, holding my hand out for him to shake. "I'm Dana."

"Austin," he says, shaking my hand firmly, but not doing the dick-guy thing of trying to crush my fingers. "Nice to meet you."

"And you. Did Carole mention anything about Lila's needs when she made the reservation?"

Austin shakes his head. "If she did, it didn't get passed on to me. Danica's a great photographer, but she's a little disorganized and her mom who is filling in on the reception desk isn't much better."

I smile gently. "And you've stepped into this as a relief pitcher?"

He shrugs, muscles rippling under a loose, white linen shirt he's wearing untucked over black jeans that are neither baggy nor tight. They're gently worn and break just right over his Docs. No pointy-tipped loafers for Austin. No designer jeans. I've never noticed his personal style before—which might be because I usually see him in a leather chest harness and G-string—but I like it.

"Danica's a friend," he explains.

And he's a good friend, covering for her. But one of the frequent problems submissives have is being taken advantage of because they're innate people-pleasers. I hope that's not happening here, but I already suspect it is.

"How long is this temp gig for?" I ask.

A slight frown beetles the smooth, deep-brown skin between Austin's brows, which are neither plucked nor a jungle. He's smooth-shaven, his black curls cropped tight to his head with a fade from his ears to his temples that's stylish but not excessive. Everything about him is contained, quiet, pleasing. How could I not have noticed him before?

"Probably two weeks," he says. "Danica has the flu."

I've taken off the week before and week after Lila's wedding. I have wedding things to do with Lila each day, but to keep her from becoming stressed, I've scheduled them between one and four, which is her best time. I have a rare free morning every day for the next two weeks.

"Let's talk afterwards about what organizational help you might need, because it doesn't seem like mom out there is up to the task. In the meanwhile, before Carole comes over to tell you she wants the red room of pain, Lila's on the spectrum. Please be patient, particularly when you're giving her directions about positions. Also, she doesn't do well being touched by people she doesn't know."

Austin's dark eyes flick from me to my sister, who is completing her third rotation around the chair: headrest, arms, seat.

"I don't generally touch my subjects, especially when they're in lingerie," he says, cracking a bright smile. "It would be great if you could tell me if my directions are confusing. Maybe we could start with your shoot while Lila's doing her makeup?"

"Oh." I glance at Carole, who is rearranging furniture in the red velvet set like she owns the place. "I wasn't going to have a shoot. This is Lila's present."

"Pretty sure the booking is for three."

My smile tightens. "Is it? And has Carole already paid?" At Austin's nod, I sigh. "Okay, I'll go first. Give me a minute to get changed."

"Great. Can I make some suggestions about settings?"

"Of course."

"Lila might like the woodland set. Her hair and skin will look amazing against the gold and green and there are some textures in there she might enjoy."

Lila loves fairies, pixies, anything elfin and otherworldly. I wouldn't have thought about how her dark hair and olive complexion would look against that backdrop, but she'll love the results.

"Perfect," I say. "Although I'm fairly sure Carole is going to want her in the red room."

Austin grins. "I can do both. And can I persuade you to do your shoot in the bedroom set? I can show you how to throw the gauze so it billows out from your body. The effect is beautiful."

"Sure. We're in your hands."

"I won't let you down, Muh-Dana." He catches himself before it's even really a fumble, but his dark cheeks stain red and he lowers his eyes to the comfortable shoes I wore today because Carole wanted to drag us around shopping before the photoshoot.

"I know you won't," I say, injecting an edge of authority into my voice.

His head lifts sharply and his pupils dilate.

"I'll be right back," I tell him.

I tap the makeup counter that runs along the edge of the mirror to get Lila's attention. When she takes out her earbud, I say, "I'm just going to get changed. I'll do my shoot first, then you, if that's okay?"

My sister's sweet, slightly wicked grin, edged in the purple lipstick that she loves and no one but my sister could make wearable on a Monday afternoon, peeps out. "You've given in? You're doing the shoot after all?"

I shoot a dark glance in Carole's direction. She's draping a red velvet throw over a red velvet armchair. Just no.

"The monster-in-law has paid for all three of us."

As always, when I call Carole the monster-in-law, Lila grins like a loon. She thinks it's hilarious. When I'm not feeling quite so judgmental, Carole's not a bad person. She's just *a lot*. A lot that Lila doesn't need. Fortunately, Lila's fiancée is one of the best people on Earth and he manages his mother deftly most of the time. It's just with the wedding so close that she's run a little wild.

"Good," Lila says before popping her ear bud back in. "You need to relax. You're turning into sister-of-the-bridezilla."

I am not. I just don't want anxiety to ruin this experience for her, so I've taken on more than the sister-of-the-bride and maid-of-honor might ordinarily do.

I stick my tongue out at her and hear a *click*.

I look in the direction of the sound. Austin lowers the camera from his face. I lift an eyebrow at him.

He blushes again, adorably, but doesn't apologize or delete the picture. I like his temerity.

"That better not go any further," I tell him.

"Personal collection," he responds with a wink.

I let my eyebrow convey what I think of that as I go off to change.

Walking around in front of my sister's mother-in-law in black satin and lace is not my idea of a good time. Added to which, Carole does not approve of either my choice in lingerie or the body I've put it on. When I walk out of the changing cubicle and over to the bedroom set, she follows, clicking her tongue.

"Black really isn't the best choice for your skin tone, dear," she says. "That midnight blue set was so lovely on you. And the padded bustier gave you some oomph."

Tough. My wardrobe choices are black cotton, black silk, black leather, and black vinyl. I'm so known for wearing black that Lila decided on a black and white theme for the wedding to avoid the inevitable argument about the maid of honor dress color. There's no point in me buying any other color.

I don't need "oomph," whatever that is. I don't have my sister's enviable curves. Or Carole's, for that matter. I've always been stick straight. I don't see any point in trying to disguise that fact with padding. My body is what it is.

I rarely hear a submissive complain. Of course, I'd beat it out of them if they did.

Austin's certainly not complaining as he fastens his fancy camera onto a tripod positioned near the edge of the bedroom set. His hands move with the assurance of long practice but he keeps his eyes on mine as I perch on the edge of the bed.

"Carole," he says. "Would you like to get changed and do your makeup while I work with Dana for a few minutes?"

"Oh." Carole pats at her face. Her makeup looks fine to me, but she'll undoubtedly spend twenty minutes touching it up. "Yes, I will."

She turns and moves off toward the changing cubicle at a power-walk.

Austin winks at me.

"Deftly done," I tell him, keeping my voice too low for Carole to hear.

"I have a lot of practice keeping difficult people happy," he says as he checks the camera's screen. I don't know much about cameras, but I can see this one's much fancier than the camera in my phone.

"Do you? Hmm. Sounds like a tough job."

He looks up and meets my eyes. "Best job in the world."

He's not talking about photography.

Pleased, I smile at him.

He moves the tripod several times before he says, "Would you stand at the end of the bed, pick up the curtains, and throw them to the side as though you were opening a pair of doors?"

Feeling only slightly ridiculous, I grab two handfuls of the gauze curtains framing the end of the bed and toss them to my sides.

Austin chuckles. "I can't help but feel your heart wasn't in that . . . Ma'am."

I give him the look that deserves. "Would you like me to try again?"

"Yes, ma'am. But first, close your eyes. Envision the room you're walking into. What waits for you there."

I envision Austin, in his club gear. The chest harness highlighting his bulging muscles, gleaming with sweat and trembling slightly. The G-string failing to contain his dripping erection. I imagine him on his knees, a ball gag in his mouth. He looks up at me with those liquid, hot chocolate eyes. Simmering for me. Melting for me.

I open my eyes and meet his. They're exactly as I imagined.

"Try again, ma'am," he says, his voice dropping to a deep rasp.

I take up the curtains again, drawing them across my body as I spread my legs and throw my shoulders back, imagining walking into that room, commanding that room. I want his first sight of me to be overwhelming. I want him on his knees not just in desire, but in supplication. In awe.

As I am constantly in awe of the trust submissives place in me.

I throw aside the curtains in a storm of clicking.

"Perfect," Austin breathes.

I grab a curtain and draw it back across my body as I imagine turning around him, drawing a veil of desire and perhaps a touch of fear over him. What will I do to him? Will I hurt him? Will I mark all that beautiful, smooth skin? Will I make him writhe and moan at my feet? Will I deny him the pleasure he wants? Will I humiliate him before I grant him the release he needs?

I throw aside the curtain and let everything I imagine pour through my eyes. Yes, yes, I will do all of that to him. I will give him everything he wants, everything he so desperately needs, but I will make him crawl and beg and ache first.

Austin grabs the camera off the tripod and moves with me as I stalk around the bed, clicking constantly. Even though he's much taller than I am, I bear down on him. Even though his face is hidden behind the camera, I push my dominance through that lens, into his eyes, into his brain.

He drops onto one knee, panting, the camera click-click-clicking as I stand over him. I am in control. I am the predator here, and he is my prey.

The clicking stops. The camera drops. He stares up at me, his eyes wet and vulnerable.

"Mistress," he whispers.

I cup his chin. "I'll expect you in the Blue Harem Room tomorrow night at nine."

"Yes, ma'am."

I nod and step back. I can't take this any further here, now, but tomorrow night, I'll make everything we just imagined together come true. "Are we done?"

He nods and picks up the camera off the carpet with trembling fingers. "Those are the best pictures I've ever taken," he murmurs.

"Good boy," I say very, very softly. "Now do my sister justice and I'll reward you tomorrow night."

He blinks up at me and smiles. "Yes, ma'am."

a buzzy tail

MASTER THEO AND ANNABELLE – ANNABELLE

THE WORDS I dread hearing the most drop from between Master Theo's curved lips.

"You lose, Annabelle."

My gut drops even as I shiver through toe-curling contractions from the motion of his fingers inside me.

He smooths my sweaty, tangled curls back from my face. "Worth it?"

"Yuh-yes, sir," I say, figuring that's what he wants to hear. What man doesn't want to hear that the orgasm he's given you is worth the bet you've just lost?

"Your eyes say you're not sure."

I sigh as he slides his fingers out of me and wipes my own wetness on my thighs. Now comes the part I hate. The aftermath. Where I'm sweaty and sticky and regretful.

"I haven't done many erotic humiliation scenes, sir," I admit, looking up at the ceiling as my body spirals downward. "I'm not sure how it will work."

He chuckles as he stretches out on the bed beside me. We're in the Blue Harem room at the club. The aquamarine drapes that give the room its name hang from the ceiling above me, filtering the room's light into something soft and romantic. Not always in keeping with what goes on in the room, which has less to do with romance and more to do with undeniable desires.

At least for me.

"It will work like every other scene, sweet thing," he says. "I'll tell you what to do and you'll obey me. Or not, in which case I get to punish you."

I try not to shudder. Master Theo is one of the club's sadists and for a service submissive like me, his punishments are something to be avoided, if not feared.

He sees my half-controlled response. "You really are feeding my beast tonight."

He runs a finger down between my bare breasts and circles my navel. He's still dressed in a black cotton shirt and jeans while I'm naked except for my panties, which are tangled around my ankles. A state of affairs which sums up my experience at the club: I'm always naked, in a state of disarray, while the masters and mistresses erotically torturing me are composed and invulnerable.

When I applied to be a house submissive, I had this ideal of submission. Of kneeling at my dominant's feet, serene, exotically beautiful, and somehow, fragrant.

The sweaty reality has been very different. Playing at private parties and New York's underground sex clubs hadn't prepared me for how much the Blunts dominants would enjoy destroying any shred of composure and leaving me a quivering mess.

"D'you need another minute to recover or should we get started?"

I've given up the idea of enjoying the afterglow with any of the club dominants except Mistress Dana and Master Javier, both of whom are big believers in wallowing in the 'glow. Some of the Masters even enjoy ruining orgasms, which is turning into a soft limit for me. I want to be relaxed after a scene, not screaming with frustration.

"I'm ready, sir," I tell him.

He gives me a speculative look. "I think a scene or two about communicating honestly with your dominant might be in your future, sweetheart. But for now, I'll take that at face value. Pull up your panties while I get an accessory or two."

I do as I'm told, sliding off the bed and sinking into the basic kneeling position all house submissives are taught while Theo gets busy in a corner. When he returns, he hands me a vintage, leather satchel. I take it from his hands and hold it open while he loads it with three vibrators and three graduated butt plugs. The largest one is ridiculously big, as large as my fist. He turns on the vibrators, closes and latches the satchel, and motions me to my feet.

"You can go anywhere within the club," he tells me. "You can speak to anyone. You offer them the satchel and ask them to guess what's inside. If they guess right, you curtsey and give them a vibrator. If they guess wrong, you offer them a butt plug. When you run out of vibrators or have the biggest butt plug in, scene's over."

I glance down at the bag in terror. Will that monster even fit inside me? "Sir, I've never taken a plug that big."

He reaches around to pat my ass. "First time for everything."

I've thought many times about refusing a Dom's command. Not using my safe word, but just telling my Dom to get fucked. The words are in my mouth.

But I keep my lips sealed over them. Theo pats my ass again. "Club closes in five hours."

I might need all that time for someone to work that monster thing into my ass.

I square my shoulders and hold the buzzing bag against my stomach, letting my muffin top jiggle with the vibration. In that sense, the club's been good for me. While my ex-husband never had anything nice to say about my body, I'm in reasonable shape for having had my fortieth birthday last year, especially for having had a desk job for twenty years. But compared to the other house submissives, particularly the young ones like Pence or the dancers like Skye and DirtyGurl, my body's soft and jiggly. Matronly.

Any self-consciousness I had about that fact was beaten out of me before I finished my first week as a house submissive. Not only did running around barely clothed destroy my inhibitions, but without exception the Doms made it clear how much they liked my curves, even the wiggly ones.

I curtsey to Theo before I take my buzzing burden to the door and let myself out into the corridor. Theo trails me like a tall, dark-haired shadow.

As I approach the dungeon reception desk, Charlotte, another of the house submissives, lifts her head and gives me her slow, sweet smile.

"Dear, where are Mistress Dana and Master Javier?"

I call all of the house submissives "dear." They are dear to me. Another way the club's been good for me is to make me feel like part of a community of subbies. I don't get along with all of the house submissives, but many of them feel like old friends.

"Mistress Dana is in the Medical Suite and Master Javier said he was going to the Library but I'm not sure whether he ended up there," Char tells me.

After a quick check of the huge, digital whiteboard hanging behind Charlotte, I go up on my tip-toes to lean across the huge reception surround so I can peck her on the cheek. I'm sure she notices the buzzing bag—it's hard to miss—but she doesn't say anything, just gives Theo a curtsey as we walk away.

Theo walks beside me down the quiet, carpeted corridor as I head toward the Library. The club is so well soundproofed that there may be submissives screaming their heads off in agony or ecstasy behind each of the doors lining the corridor, but you'd never know it out in the hallway. Out here, there's nothing but peace and the elegance of the club's classic décor.

"Why Dana and Javier, sweetheart?" Theo asks as we pad barefoot over the rich, Oriental carpeting. There's something equalizing about us both being barefoot. We could be friends instead of dominant and submissive. But I'm not sure I could ever call any of the club's sadists "friends." Dana and Javier are maybe the closest I'll ever come.

"I trust them," I say simply.

"And for the third?" he asks.

I shrug. I have a surprise in mind for him. A way to maybe win the game after all. But I don't want to give it away yet. "I'll have to see who I can find," I say.

"Do you trust any of the other club members?" he asks, a frown creasing his brow.

Not yet. There are a few who seem trustworthy, like Master Logan, but I'm not sure of yet. Overall, they seem okay but there's some niggle of doubt. Like Master Logan withdrawing from the club for six months and leaving the house submissives to fend for themselves under the not-so-benevolent neglect of Master Ryan. Club gossip says he had his reasons for ghosting us, but once doubt's been planted, I find it hard to overcome.

Theo himself falls into that category. As a Dom, despite his worrisome penchant for denying orgasms, he seems conscientious and considerate. But the subbie grapevine is whispering about how he treated DirtyGurl after she was attacked by a trio of thugs. She's a kickboxer and got away from them herself, but he interrogated her like she was the perp rather than the victim. I've had too many dealings with the police myself not to believe that rumor.

"I only know Dana and Javier well," I say instead.

Theo humphs.

I turn right at the end of the corridor, into a long portrait gallery with an intricate, parquet floor. Hunts are often held in here, with visitors as the "hounds" and a house submissive or two as the "fox." I haven't been picked to be a fox yet, but I've been memorizing all the ducts and secret passageways that the club is riddled with, for the day that I am. I switch the vibrating bag to my left hand and rub the bald pate of every marble and bronze bust I pass. It's a club superstition and I can use all the luck I can get tonight.

I do not want to end the night with that giant plug in my butt.

Another heavy, paneled door at the end of the gallery opens into the club's huge library. The space soars up two stories, with a mezzanine level and a giant, crystal chandelier presiding over it all. Every wall of the library is lined with floor to ceiling bookshelves. Rolling steps help the vertically challenged reach the highest shelves. The books, ranging from leather-bound classics to yellow-jacketed paperbacks, aren't just for show. I've passed several happy afternoons curled up in one of the comfortable armchairs reading from the club's extensive collection.

Tonight, I'm not looking for a book, but for the master who sits in one of the deep armchairs, his feet propped on the back of a submissive kneeling on all fours in front of him. To a casual observer, it would look like Master Javier is ignoring the man at his feet, but I see that Javier holds his newspaper just that bit higher so he can keep his dark eyes on the sweating sub even while he reads.

Javier's unquestionably one of the club's scariest sadists, but he's also given me the most tender, attentive aftercare I've ever had.

I approach his chair and kneel, setting the humming bag in front of me. I keep my eyes down but my chin up, the way he's taught me.

"Nicely done, Annabelle," Javier says after a minute. His voice is like a good whiskey: deep, smooth, with the perfect amount of bite and burn.

"Good evening, sir," I respond.

"Is this a social visit or have you brought me something?"

I pick up the bag and offer it to him. "Please guess what's inside, sir."

Instead of taking the bag, Javier rearranges his feet, crossing one ankle over another, and turns a page of his newspaper.

"Mmm, what do I get if I guess correctly?"

"The gift of a vibrator, sir." Theo didn't say I couldn't be honest about the terms of my task.

"And what do I get if I guess incorrectly?"

"The gift of a butt plug, sir." Theo also didn't say I had to conceal the forfeit.

Javier turns another page. "And the gift of a submissive to use said plug on?"

"Yes, sir."

"Mmm. That's a generous gift." He lowers the edge of the newspaper and looks at Theo, standing a foot or two behind me. "I wouldn't have guessed you'd be so generous, Master Theo."

Theo chuckles.

Javier returns to his newspaper and reads another page before he says, "Which would you like me to choose, mon chou?"

I made the mistake of giving him a subbie platitude the first time he did a scene with me. My ass regretted it for several hours. I've been careful to give him the unvarnished truth ever since. Something I appreciate about both Javier and Dana is that they recognize the gift of unfiltered honesty.

"Both, sir."

"Ah." Javier licks his finger and turns another page of the paper. "Very well. I guess there are both vibrators and butt plugs in the bag. I'll take my vibrator now and claim the further reward of a scene with you on your next available shift involving said vibrator."

Grinning, I open the bag and hand him one of the buzzing vibrators. It's a plain, flesh-colored, plastic stick. Javier immediately flicks the switch to turn it off and waves it at Theo. "Disappointingly pedestrian. Next time, at least provide a rabbit."

"You don't like my pick of fake penis, get your own," Theo says.

Javier turns glittering eyes and a white smile on me. "I'll find something better to torment you with, ma belle, never fear. I'll only make you suffer from pleasure, not from your Dom's execrable selection in sex toys."

I bite down on my lower lip to keep from giggling. Javier's caustic sense of humor is one of the many joys of doing scenes with him.

Javier flicks his little finger at me before going back to his paper.

"Off with you, minette. Don't forget to text me the time of our next rendezvous."

"Yes, sir."

"Be an angel and give my submissive a kiss before you go so he knows what a perfect footstool he is."

"Yes, sir."

I shift the bag aside so I can get down to the living footstool's level. Cappa lifts his dark head, the muscles of his neck bunching with strain. He's sweating so hard his hair hangs in strings across his forehead. I wonder how long he's been kneeling like this, how heavy Javier's feet must feel on his back by now.

I duck my head to relieve his strain and, very gently, press my lips to his.

Cappa smiles at me before lowering his head.

I don't ask him if he's okay. It would be rude to Javier to question his handling of his submissive. It might also break the mood of the scene. Like me, Cappa has a safe word if the physical rigors of the scene get to be too much. I don't know if he's as reluctant to use his safe word as I am, but he has one.

Pleased with the outcome of my first maneuver, I rise, collect the satchel, bow to Master Javier, and trot back through the library.

Theo stretches his legs and keeps pace with me. "I should have set the terms more carefully, shouldn't I?"

I give him a small smile. Now's not the time to get overconfident.

But my ass is feeling a little safer.

Next stop is the medical suite. I checked the scene board after Charlotte told me where Mistress Dana was to ensure that it wasn't a closed scene. It's not and there are five people in the large, sterile, white room. Austin, another house submissive, is lying on one of the stainless-steel, medical-examination tables. His thickly muscled arms and legs are slack, hanging off the edges of the table. His huge chest rises and falls with slow, even breaths. His face is turned away from me, but even at this angle, I can see the way his beatific smile rounds his cheeks.

That's the smile of a happy submissive.

Dana's the only Domme who has asked me to do scenes with her. She's the only woman I've ever had sex with. And it looks like she's off the market. Although she's been a club member for over two years—and Austin's been a house submissive for a lot longer—she never did scenes with him. That changed a few weeks ago. I'm not sure what brought him to her notice, but she noticed him in a very big way. Although neither has mentioned exclusivity, they only have eyes for each other.

Which is unfortunate, because Dana is a phenomenal Domme. I often have trouble getting out of my own way enough to reach subspace. Dana got me there in record time and helped me stay there, keeping me focused on the scene whenever I started to let anything else creep in.

And the sex was eye-opening. I've never felt a strong attraction to another woman. Looking at women, I still don't feel the quickening in my blood, the tightening in my belly, which I feel when I meet an attractive man. But for sex that good, I'll take a second look.

Dana glances at me as I enter. As do the other spectators: Masters Karl and Franco, and Mistress Maude, who are seated in chairs near the door so they can watch the scene without getting in the way.

There's a lot of Big D energy in the room. And by "Big D" I mean dominance. All of the dominants are sadists and I can only imagine what Dana did to Austin to satisfy the collective lust for pain in the room. She's wiping off some very scary-looking tools and placing them on a rolling stand as I enter.

Despite the intimidation factor of the crackling Big D energy and the frightening tools, I walk into the room, stop a few paces from Dana, and kneel.

Although we only did a few scenes, I remember perfectly how Dana wanted me to kneel. Shoulders back. Head down. Eyes down. I place the buzzing bag in front of me and assume the position.

Then I wait. Dana makes me wait much longer than Javier did. But she's more involved in post-scene mechanics than he was. After she finishes cleaning the tools, she walks around Austin several times, her black stilettos clicking over the white floor tile. On the third circle, she stops in front of me and taps the top of my head.

"Good evening, Annabelle," she says. She's still using her Domme voice, both throaty and cold.

"Good evening, Mistress Dana." Since she's given me the signal to look up, I do, taking in those towering heels and the black catsuit stretched tight over Dana's slender curves.

"Do you have something for me in that noisy bag?"

"I do, ma'am. Please guess what's inside."

Her laugh has less bite than her tone. I've heard that before. After a scene's over, she mellows. If she wasn't a Domme, I could see enjoying Girls' Nights Out with Dana.

"Not much of a challenge to guess what's making it so noisy," she says. "So there has to be more to it than that."

"Yes, ma'am," I say, because she impressed on me the importance of answering her verbally during our scenes.

She looks off to the doorway behind me. "One of your games, Theo?" she asks.

Theo grunts.

"I see. I guess a vibrator and butt plug or two," Dana says.

I can't keep myself from smiling. That's the other reason I came to find Dana. She's smarter than the whips she wields.

"Correct, ma'am." I take a vibrator out of the bag and offer it to her with a seated curtsey.

Dana inclines her head at me. She takes the small, purple bullet from my hands, turns it off with a click, and rolls it in her long fingers.

"Thank you," she says to me. "A vibrator's always the perfect gift for every occasion."

She winks at me. An even wider smile breaks across my face.

"May I rise, ma'am?"

"Yes, good girl," she says. Praise is never absent-minded with

Dana. She's very focused, and when that focus is on you, it's hard not to preen under that laser-like regard.

Glowing, I push up to my feet and curtsey to her again.

Before Theo can devise something to ruin my success, I turn to him and curtsey. "Good evening, Master Theo. Please guess what's in the bag?"

His eyes flare before he narrows them. "Well played, sweetheart."

Dana laughs huskily. "Did she beat you at your own game, Theo? What did you lose?"

"The pleasure of seeing her take a four-inch plug."

Dana laughs again and her laugh is echoed around the room.

Mistress Maude unfolds herself from a chair near the door, brushing down her silk dress before patting me on the shoulder. "Good job, dear. Never let a man get the better of you." She winks before she sweeps out of the room.

Theo growls after her.

"Is the scene over, sir?" I ask.

He crosses his arms over his chest. "Looks that way. I'll be more careful how I word things next time."

I finally let a victorious smile break across my face. "I'll look forward to it, sir."

a friendly tail

CAPPA AND CHARLOTTE – CAPPA

"CAP?" Charlotte pokes her head around the doorway of the dimly-lit dungeon.

I glance up and nod. "Hey, Char."

"Master Karl just called. He's had a family emergency. He can't make it."

I set down the flogger I was oiling. "Well, crap."

Charlotte slides into the room, a pale, slender shadow outlined in black lace and topped with a dark crown that she's tortured into curls today. I don't know why she bothers. She looks better with the smooth bob she usually wears.

But I suppose with the curls, we're easier to tell apart.

The Doms and subs of Blunts like to say that Charlotte and I are twins. We're in no way related, but we share the same height and build and coloring. And it's fun to play with. We even talked Brenna, a former house submissive who runs her own tattoo parlor, to give us matching rosary and crucifix tattoos on our left arms, since we both come from Catholic families who have rejected our life choices.

Charlotte perches on the edge of the bed where I was hoping to get thoroughly fucked after the flogging. Fuck, I'm horny. I love Master Logan. I mean, I really love Master Logan. And I know he doesn't feel the same way about me and I know I shouldn't be as attached to him as I am since he's committed to my friend Emily, but I can't seem to stop myself. I love his dominance and I worship him for the way he's stepped in to top me after everything spun out of control. But he won't touch me any way that isn't purely platonic and sometimes I just need to be fucked.

Looks like that's not happening tonight.

Char picks up my phone and taps the app I have playing the modern jazz Master Karl likes. "Mind if I change this over?"

"Knock yourself out, doll."

She switches it over to a local indie band we both like and I roll my shoulders to the beat. Nothing against Master Karl, but modern jazz will never be my thing. I begin hanging the floggers I'd taken out back on a rolling rack to tuck them away since they aren't going to get any use tonight. The music lifts my mood a little and by the end of the song, I'm swinging my hips to the beat.

Once I finish putting away the floggers, I move to the sex swing I'd pulled into the middle of the room and start pushing it on its overhead track back toward the wall.

"Before you put that away," Charlotte says, her tone soft and hesitant, "could I convince you to use it tonight?"

"Huh?"

I look over to where she's sitting. She's tucked into herself, knees pulled up, arms wrapped around them. I must have been blind to miss her body language when she came in, too involved in my disappointment. I abandon the sex swing and cross the room to sit next to her. I slide my arm around her shoulders and hug her to my side.

"What happened?"

She tips her head onto my shoulder. "Nothing I shouldn't have expected. War's gone back to his wife—"

"Again? Char, why do you keep letting him string you along? He's a dick. He's not going to leave her. Every time he goes back to her, you spiral. Cut him the fuck loose."

She sighs. "He's familiar. He's safe. He doesn't ask too much of me."

"Babe." I give her shoulders a squeeze. I know this is a constant point of tension for Charlotte, and the other house submissives who aren't pain-sluts like I am. A lot of the club Doms are sadists and some of them have difficulty adjusting the level of play they need to satisfy their inner beast to what a service submissive like Char can comfortably handle. Which leaves the service submissives dancing the line of pushing themselves to take too much or feeling like they haven't satisfied their tops. "Has anyone—?"

She shakes her head quickly. "No, nothing like that. But with Masters Martin, Ty, and Harte off fishing, no one has booked scenes with me this week, either."

"Aww." I squeeze her again. "Are you feeling lonely, doll?"

She nods. "I just want something friendly and safe."

I can do friendly and safe. Charlotte and I would never work for anything else. I can switch when I need to, but I quickly spiral without a strong dominant, and Char's so submissive her first thought every morning must be, "how can I serve you?"

"Well, I don't know," I tease her. "Have you been a good girl and earned a friendly, safe ride on Cappa's swing?"

She elbows me. "You owe me a million, all the times I've subbed on the desk for you."

Very true. Between Master Javier, who likes to flex by calling me off the desk to serve him, and a run of bad luck at the underground clubs that left me with too many stitches to work for over a week, I owe Charlotte a large number of favors. But admitting that's too easy.

"So you're trying to bribe your way onto Cappa's swing," I say, deadpan.

She knows I'm teasing her and giggles. "I'm going to call it your swing from now on."

"At least I have enough to swing," I say, referring to another house submissive we both know and dislike who doesn't have anything to brag about down there. "Red and yellow okay or are we doing safe, friendly, and vanilla?"

"Definitely red and yellow," Char says, telling me she wants this to be a scene. Which works for me. I'm over Master Karl standing me up now and getting into the idea of doing a scene with Charlotte. She may not be a pain-slut, but she has serious humiliation and praise kinks. I can work with those. I can more than work with those.

"Mmm, you need to earn a ride on Cappa's swing. How about you crawl across the room and back? Every five steps, take off an item of clothing. Top, down."

Char's pretty brown eyes, framed with thick, natural lashes that are the envy of every woman and many of the men at the club, widen. "Yes . . . what should I call you?"

Nothing fits a switch. It's the perennial problem. Having someone call me "master" or "sir" makes me feel like an utter fraud.

"Mighty C," I say, to keep this light and playful.

She giggles wildly as she slides off the bed. "Yes, Mighty C."

I may be a switch. I may crave submitting more than I'll ever enjoy topping. But fuck if there isn't something awesome about seeing someone get down on their hands and knees because I told them so.

We're all taught how to crawl prettily, pleasingly. Crossing one knee in front of the other so our backsides sway. But Charlotte does it particularly well, sliding sinuously over the carpet. She's wearing the house submissive uniform of basque, G-string, suspenders, and fishnet stockings. She took off her stilettos and left them by the door when she came in, which we're also trained to do unless the top has asked us to wear our heels. Easier on both the dungeon floors and our ankles. Her sweet toes curl as she crawls.

She stops and removes the headband she's wearing, setting it aside out of her path. I grin at her back. She's into this. She could have started with her basque set and stripped off in twenty paces. I wouldn't have argued. Instead, she's drawing it out. I sprawl back onto my elbows, stretching out my legs and letting my enjoyment show in the tent in my own G-string, as I watch her.

"Your buttocks, something in me reaches. More delectable than a pair of peaches," I say in a sing-song.

Char collapses forward onto her elbows, giggling. "That's so bad."

"Your poetry is perfect and praiseworthy, Mighty C," I quip at her.

"Your poetry is as perfect as my delectable buttocks, Mighty C."

It's my turn to laugh. "I guess I don't have Master Martin's silver tongue," I admit, referring to the club's resident poet. He's won awards and everything. He never writes poetry about our asses, though. Major failing in my eyes.

"You have a golden tongue," she says, throwing a flirty glance over her shoulder before she starts crawling again.

I waggle it at her, which sets her off giggling again as she stops and takes off the lace collar framing her throat. She doesn't remove the leather collar under it that's the mate of mine and every other house submissive's. I wouldn't ever ask her to. There are a few subbies who treat their club collar like nothing, but for most of us, it's a symbol of the belonging we've sought and dreamed about all our lives.

Since we're just having fun and I'm not a real Dom who might be too proud to get on his knees, I slide off the bed, cross the floor, and kneel behind her. "Cheek to the carpet," I tell her.

She immediately follows my command, getting her ass in the air. I peel down her G-string just enough to expose her bare lips, sheened from how much she's enjoying the scene, and put my golden tongue to work. I'm not afraid of getting into it. Seven years at the club has cured me of any inhibitions. I lick and suck and nibble until she's slick from slit to crack and squealing her first orgasm into the carpet.

Before she comes down and stimulation becomes too much, I slap her wet pink lips with my open palm a dozen times. Her back jerks up into the air as she has a fast clitoral orgasm. She sags onto her belly. I slide my forearm under her hips to help keep her in position. I won't punish her the way a real Dom would for breaking position, but she shouldn't get into bad habits.

Once she starts to recover, she realizes what she's done and gets back on her hands and knees with her cheek to the floor. "Thank you, Mighty C," she whispers.

"You're welcome, doll. Keep going."

I release her and cross to the trolly of scenes supplies to find a wipe. I clean up, then get back on the bed to watch the rest of the show.

She's nice and relaxed from the orgasm and it shows in the roll of her shoulders and hips, the soft blush staining her cheeks and chest as she turns around at the far end of the dungeon and begins crawling back toward me, her pretty breasts hanging free after she removes her basque. I push my own G-string aside and palm my dick until it's standing straight up and jerking with each heart-beat.

"You look gorgeous," I tell her. "You're going to get fucked so hard. Anywhere you're sore?"

Fluttering those midnight lashes at me, she shakes her head. "I'm yours wherever you want me."

That's an invitation to anal if I ever heard one. "Yes, you are. Stop and squeeze your nipples for me."

She does, sitting back on her heels the way we're taught. Her movement's graceful, natural, totally unselfconscious. Everyone has their own beauty, at least in my mind. But I think Charlotte might be the most underrated sub at Blunts other than DirtyGurl. DirtyGurl's rough and tough and maybe even a little stained on the outside. You have to get past that to see the beauty she hides inside.

Charlotte's beautiful inside and out. She's just so quiet and unassuming that most Doms look past her to flashier beauties like Apple, Skye, and Fleur. Even Briar Rose, as much of a bitch as she is, gets more scenes than Char. The only Dom who consistently books time with Charlotte is Master Harold, which makes no sense to me because he's very solidly gay. But he often books her for whole week-ends. Maybe she's doing his laundry or something to feed her need to serve? I don't know. I've asked her and all she'll say is that he's very kind to her and he's asked her not to talk about their scenes.

I could try to work her down into subspace with a few more orgasms and see if she'd tell me then. That's something some of the Blunts Doms do. I've always thought it was a dirty trick and after hearing Master Logan talk to his friend Niall about the suppression of the superego in subspace, I realize ethical Doms feel this way, too.

So instead of satisfying my curiosity at the expense of my sub, I stroke my dick, lick my lips, and watch the beautiful girl pinching her nipples until they flush as red as her bitten lips.

"Feel that all the way down in your clit, doll?" I ask, squeezing my tip until I'm as flushed as she is.

She nods. "Yes, Mighty C."

"Good girl. You're such a good girl, Char. You follow instructions so well. You do everything so prettily. Crawl for me and when you reach the bed, suck on me for a minute as a reward for being such a wonderful subbie."

The rose staining her cheeks darkens and her pupils expand. It's counterintuitive that giving someone a blowjob would be a reward, but I know from personal experience that it is. Knowing you've pleased your top so much they want your mouth on their body—it fills a subbie's soul.

She crawls forward, stops and takes off her lacy suspender belt and wiggles it off her hips, before crawling again. She's down to just her stockings by the time she reaches me. I decide to have her leave them on. They're a fun texture to press into her skin when we're fucking.

"So good, Char," I say as she kneels between my feet. "Leave your fishnets on and suck me. Do you want me to wear a condom, doll?"

She shakes her head. We're tested constantly and almost all club members—male and female—are on birth control, but I always check. It's more than polite. It shows my sub they're safe and cared for. Master Javier does it every time we scene, even though he's been doing scenes with me for years. He'd never fall for me, so I haven't let myself fall for him—much—but I appreciate his dominance like nothing else.

I haven't given her any instruction beyond sucking me and Charlotte doesn't innovate during scenes. She does exactly what she's told. I angle my dick toward her, pushing down on my base with my thumb while cupping my balls. She takes my tip into her mouth delicately and immediately gives me enough suction to hollow her cheeks. I shift so I can cup her face with my free hand.

"Such a good girl. Give it to me nice and hard. Make my balls draw up."

She does, pulling so strongly my eyes cross. It's just on the right side of too much. Too hard. My tip throbs in protest against her hard palate. Fuck, so good. I groan and praise her. "Doll, sweet doll. Suck on me until I go blind. Just like that. Your mouth is a miracle, Char."

All of the house submissives are used to giving vigorous head. A lot of the Doms like it. I'm more used to giving than I am getting, but I am not complaining as she sucks and sucks and sucks, blowing out huge breaths through her nose in counterpoint to each draw. When I'm panting as hard as she is and sure she's about to pull my brains out through my dick, I stroke her cheek. "Into the swing, babe. You're so good I'm gonna come soon. I want to feel you all around me when I blow."

With a gasp, she releases me and sits back. "Damn you can take it hard, Cap. Half the Masters here would be screaming if I sucked them that hard."

I chuck her under the chin. "Years of CBT, doll."

Staggering a little, I rise and help her up. I wish I was as strong as Master Logan or Master Ty so I could scoop her up and carry her to the swing. I have to settle for pinching her ass and chasing her to it. She climbs in nimbly. She knows where to grab the chains and how to get her knee into the back support before she tries to sit. I barely have to help her at all. Once she's in and reclining, I adjust the swing's back to a fifteen-degree angle, which is what I find comfortable. I stroke her calves before I guide her legs up and clamp her ankles in the overhead straps.

She wriggles as I pull her down a little in the seat so her ass overhangs it and her holes are completely exposed to me. I finger her, finding her pussy still wet and pulsing, while I check in with her.

"All good, doll?"

She shifts in the swing, getting comfortable, and wraps her hands around the chains to hold on. "All good, Mighty C."

I tickle my middle finger in her G-spot until she moans.

"Wish I'd worn my piercing, doll. Then I could give you a real massage here." I took out all my piercings and left them at home, thinking I'd be scening with Master Karl tonight. It's much too dangerous to wear metal during scenes with Karl. He's been known to tear piercings out. He'll pay for the plastic surgery afterwards. He's good like that. But that exceeds this pain-slut's tolerance, so I'm careful to take everything out.

She rolls her head back and forth on the swing's support. "I'm not complaining. Fuck me, Cap, please. I need it."

I know that need. "You got it, doll."

I rub her G-spot for another moment, until I can feel her tighten around my fingers, before slapping her clit a few times with my cock to get myself really hard again. Then I feed myself into her before grabbing the swing's hand loops. I lean back and find my balance.

"Ready?"

"Yes, yes," she moans.

I yank the swing to me as I thrust, hammering into her. She yelps on the first thrust, which means I've gone too deep. But the bite of pain does it for her. Her legs shake and she arches up off the backrest with a howl. "Oh, god, yes!"

"Mighty C," I remind her, grinning, as I work into a rhythm that rattles both our fillings.

Having been in this swing a time or two myself, I know the angle that feels best, with my legs slightly bent, using my weight to offset the movement of the swing. Charlotte's pussy is a sweet, wet constriction around my pistoning cock. It's not the same as being fucked, letting myself go, falling into another's rhythm, but there's a crazed high to this as my cock swells and pulses. My body grows tight.

There's always a tripping point for me in sex. A moment when my brain short-circuits and my body takes over. In that moment, everything in me unites in the quest for satisfaction. Nothing distracts me. Nothing diverts me. I'm going to come no matter what.

I drive and drive and drive towards that tripping point. Everything else goes away. I'm not worried about what I'm doing with Master Logan and how it could affect my friendship with Emily. I don't care that I'm a month behind in my rent. I don't give a shit that this is the third time Master Karl's stood me up. All that matters to me is coming.

Charlotte writhes against me, her legs flexing as she kicks against the ankle restraints. I wrap my hands around her thighs and pull her to me even harder as my body cranks into high gear. All my muscles go rigid. Euphoric chemicals sing their high, sweet song through my blood. My back snaps like a bowstring. The contraction of every muscle forces a long, low groan out of my chest. I go up on my toes, lifting the whole swing with me, as I pour out that unbearable tension into Charlotte's receptive body.

"Oh, oh, Cap." She reaches for me and I sag over her, letting my head drop to her chest. She strokes my hair, a little longer than hers and just starting to curl where it brushes my shoulders. I lazily mouth her nipple as I come down from the high of my orgasm.

"Beautiful, doll," I tell her.

"It was. Thank you, Mighty C." She giggles and the motion of her diaphragm pushes my softening cock out of her.

I kiss a soft spot between her breasts before lifting off her and moving to the scene cart for wipes. I clean us up and help her out of the swing. We're both a little shaky, so I guide her over to the bed and crash on my back, holding out my arm to her. She settles on her front next to me. She crosses her arms and rests her chin on them, looking at me with a gentle smile.

"You'd be a great top, you know," she says.

"And miss out on the monthly joy of Master Karl standing me up? How could I?"

She giggles. "Some of the Doms here are such assholes."

"True." I sigh and stroke her shoulder. "Master Logan and Master Mac are making an effort. If you're having problems, you should tell them."

"You really trust Master Logan after he left us?"

I blow out a breath and look at the room's plastered ceiling. I've never been in another dungeon that has Victorian crown moldings. Blunts is a strange set of dichotomies, that's for sure.

"I'm trying to," I admit. "I understand why he left. He wouldn't have done right by us if he'd been here. I'm not saying he did the right thing, because he made a commitment to us, too. But I understand why he did it. He is trying to make it right."

"Does he really even care about us? He's with Emily now. She's never even been a house submissive."

"He cares. He's topping me outside the club."

"Fuck, Cap, when did that start?"

"Couple of weeks ago. After, you know."

Her hand steals out from under her chin to brush against my side. The bruises are gone. My ribs have healed. But for a while, I looked more like an overripe eggplant than a man.

"You've been steady? You haven't been to the clubs?"

I shake my head. "I've done a couple of scenes with Doms Master Javier recommended. Substitute sadists, he called them." I snort, remembering his derision. Despite him not understanding why I'd want to go out of the club to find a top, Master Javier gave me what I needed. He's a good Dom. He gives everything but his heart. "Master Logan interviewed them first. The scenes went well."

"You're not doing scenes with Master Logan?"

"No. Platonic topping only. It's working."

"So far. You know it's a band aid."

"Yeah, I know."

She rubs my chest. "None of us really have it figured out, do we?"

"No," I admit.

With Master Logan topping me, I feel a little closer to the answers. But I know I still have a long way to go.

a queenly tail

MASTER BULL, KIKI, AND TWITCH – TWITCH

I ADJUST my crown and walk up to the club's reception desk.

I've been here many times, but always as Sir's guest. Never on my own. Never because I had a reason other than his pleasure to be here.

Dan on the reception desk signs me in with a nod of his greying head. "I'll page Maude to meet you in the library. You're early."

I could tell him a queen is never early. We're always exactly on time. But he's being nice by paging the Mistress I'm here to meet, so I just give him a megawatt smile and sail through the inner door into the club on my platform wedges.

Blunts is a throwback to another era. It's modeled on the eighteenth-century gentlemen's clubs of its founder's homeland. Not that I've been to England. Or seen the inside of a gentleman's club. But I watch *Bridgerton*. And *Sanditon*, for that matter. I mean, with all those delicious bottoms on display, who wouldn't?

I sashay down the hallway, my heels silent on the deep red, Oriental carpet. I pass one of the house submissives, Fleur. She's kneeling on a platform in one of the alcoves spaced along the hall.

Her pale skin, with its colorful tattoos that are surely the club's resident tattooist's work, is an eye-popping contrast to the dark wood paneling framing her as she poses naked, her hands bound behind her back, a tail of black fur as rich and dark as her hair peeking out from between her sculpted ass cheeks and furling around her thighs.

I know better than to speak to her, even though we're friends. I pause to give her beauty the appreciation it deserves. She smiles at me but doesn't speak. I smile back before I continue on my way to the grand staircase.

I could take the elevator up to the library. It's one of those lovely antique things with a cage that you pull across and a handle to go up and down. Bit of an adventure just to go up a floor. But I'm missing leg day and I can always use the cardio. So I run up the stairs and wait at the security door at the top for the house submissive on the reception desk to buzz me through.

Pence makes me wait longer than anyone else would. He's intimidated by my fabulousness. I covet his hair, which is better than a Kpop idol's, I'll admit, although he should dye it silver-grey like mine if he really wants to turn heads. Otherwise, he's a nasty little piece of work. How he managed to finagle a collar from Master Harold, who is one of the club's silverbacks and such a sweetheart, I'll never know.

Once Pence buzzes me through, I push the door open and take a sharp left, while adjusting my crown in his direction with my middle finger.

"You have to sign in," Pence barks after me.

I pivot like I'm still walking the catwalk and strut over to his desk. "Oh, darling, didn't anyone tell you? I work here now."

The way Pence's face falls would be comical if I wasn't well aware of his malice. I was upstate with my sister over the summer when Pence and that false queen, Rachel, ganged up on the club's little, Emily. But Kiki was in the shower and overhead the whole thing. Emily's daddy, Master Logan, got to Pence before Kiki got out, but if it had been me, I'd have jumped out in all my naked glory to snatch the brat bald for the things he said to her.

Pence pushes the papers on the reception desk around with his fingertip—unmanicured, the little heathen—before he answers me. "No one mentioned it. You're joining as a house submissive?"

I scoff gently. "As if Sir would ever share me." His eyes dilate slightly as that shot hits the mark. Master Harold may have given him a collar, but Pence is still a house submissive, so they're not exclusive the way I am with Sir and Kiki. "Our little club historian has identified holdings in need of repair. Antique books and manuscripts are my specialty." I flip a silver-gray lock over my shoulder. "So they've asked me to accept a position in the library."

"You're a librarian?" Pence asks flatly.

I chuck him under the chin with my forefinger, which you can bet has a fresh set. "Stop by the library any time, darling. I'm sure you could use a little education."

I pivot and strut away. I dressed conservatively today. A vintage 70s pantsuit in teal and black paisley and a fringed leather bolero jacket to set off my diamante crown. The pantsuit makes my legs look so long and my ass look so tight I barely got out the door before Bull ravaged me. Again.

I love knowing Pence is looking at that tight, rayon-clad ass as I walk away.

Although queens are always exactly on time, since Mistress Maude isn't waiting for me, I stroll slowly through the long gallery that leads to the library. The artwork here, particularly the statuary, isn't sufficiently appreciated by the club members. There's a smoke-stained Titian that I've begged Sir a thousand times to have restored. To say nothing about a copy of Giambologna's "Rape of the Sabine Women" that I think is an early Bartolini. Restoration and examination could prove who the sculptor is. If it is an unknown Bartolini, it's a true treasure, worth thousands. Maybe if the management committee are happy with my work in the library, they'll finally listen to me about the club's art.

At the end of the long gallery, there's an imposing, carved door into the library. I open it to the sweet sounds of fucking.

My friend Emily said she'd be available after my meeting with Mistress Maude to show me the worst of the damaged books she's found while doing research in the club's archives. I see, as I walk through and my platforms alternately clack and go silent on the library's thick area rugs, that Emily's daddy has decided to take advantage of her availability.

He's bound her over a reading desk, her hands tied with pink rope, her cheek pressed to the wood, her legs spread and ankles bound to the table's legs. She's naked except for her collar and black thigh-highs. He's thrown her dress and his suit jacket over a nearby chair and unbuttoned his shirt so I can see his chest and abs flexing as he moves, stroking slowly in and out of her small body. His leather belt is draped over her lower back; pink wheals on her pale ass and thighs show where he's used it on her. His big hand is spread over her head, fingers sunk in her dark curls, both holding her down and cradling her. With an expression of concentrated bliss, he pulls back, spreads her cheeks with his free hand, and slowly sinks into her ass.

I fan myself as I pass them. Having been in that position many time with my own Sir, I know exactly how uncomfortable it is to be restrained like that and how unbelievably good it feels to be fucked through the pain.

I wish I could take a picture of them and send it to Sir, but I know Master Logan doesn't permit images of Emily in sexual situations. There's a secure server for the club where some of the masters, including mine, allow images to be shared, but Master Franco made us all sign waivers because, as he lectured us, an image lasts forever and even with the best intentions, the club can't guarantee images won't be leaked.

I don't care who sees Sir fucking me, but Emily has a career which could be damaged by sexy snaps. So, as beautiful as I think they are, I keep my phone in my pocket.

I'm distracted from their loveliness by the books. Leather-bound books. Hardbacks with glittering gilded edges. Bright yellow paperbacks. Books so well loved their titles are indecipherable. Books so pristine they can't ever have been opened. Books from floor to ceiling. Books neatly filed on shelves. Books stacked on tables. Books, books, books, and over the faint scent of Logan and Emily fucking, the vanilla and leather of books.

I extend my arms and twirl around in the middle of the space. There's nowhere I love so much as a library. Nothing that soothes my busy mind as much as the order of stacks. No smell better than the vanillin of books.

Someone chuckles and I look back at Logan and Emily. They're still engrossed in each other. It's the statuesque woman with hair as silver as mine, only hers is natural, crossing the library on her sensible heels who is laughing. She reaches me and leans in for air-kisses, before taking my elbow and steering me toward the space under the mezzanine overhang where Emily has set up a desk for her research.

"How are you, Twitch?" Maude asks. "How's dear Kiki?"

"I'm fabulous, as always, Mistress. Kiki's recovering. Bull dotes over her like it was something serious."

I wave one hand airily. I'm being glib because Kiki doesn't want people fussing, even though it was the big C and she needed a double-mastectomy. But she *is* recovering, and we *are* doting over her like a pair of hens.

"Text me when she's ready for visitors and I'll bring Javier to antagonize Bull while we have some well-deserved time together."

"I will."

Maude's being extremely friendly and familiar today—which she isn't always—and that tells me how things are going to go. Although some of the membership committee was against hiring me because I'm not a house submissive, Maude led the charge once everyone's favorite little made a fuss. Sir used to complain, half seriously, that the house submissives treated Master Logan like a rock star. But that's nothing compared to the way most of the masters and mistresses treat Emily. They make our doting on Kiki look like benevolent neglect.

When we arrive at the space Emily's carved out for herself, I see there have been important changes. There's not one desk anymore. There are two, facing each other, handsomely outfitted with top-of-the-line laptops, ledgers, and stationary. Tucked under the wrought-iron, spiral staircase up to the mezzanine is a long, wooden table with an antique apothecary's cabinet behind it, the cubby holes filled with bookbinding equipment. There are rolls of marbled endpapers, clamps and presses of several different sizes, boxes of awls and punches, stacks of spine tape, a long strip of glittering, curved needles, even a little fume hood off to one side for the adhesive.

I clap my hands together. "Look at this!"

"Emily arranged it. She researched what you'd need for bookbinding and ordered all the supplies. If there's anything else you need, just speak to her. Logan's negotiated quite a budget. It will cover anything you'd need within reason."

"Marvelous."

I examine everything, my fingers fluttering over smooth and sharp edges. Shiny new. High quality. I haven't been short of money since Sir took me and Kiki as his submissives, but bookbinding has only been a hobby until now, so I've done it everywhere from my parents' basement to Bull's dining table and often with makeshift equipment.

"Anything else you need?" Maude asks.

"No, no." I pull out a roll of paper and spread it on the worktop, admiring the pattern. "Everything's lovely."

"Shall I leave you to get settled? Emily will be along . . . mmm, in a bit, to show you what's damaged. Chess has asked for a report at the end of the week. If I could make a suggestion, you might take a look through the catalogue and include a list of anything you and

Emily think should be added to the library. She was saying something about A. N. Roquelaure?"

"The Beauty series." I chuckle. "Kinky classics."

Maude smiles indulgently. "Well, we should certainly have a comprehensive collection of classic kink."

"I'll put it together," I assure her.

"Copy Javier and me, oh, and Logan and Bull."

"Of course. Is there . . . any issue?"

I'd understood from Sir that everything was settled, this meeting with Maude a formality. It makes my anxiety flicker that it might not be.

She pats my shoulder. "No, dear. J and I are taking a more, mmm, hands-on role in things now that Logan's returned. Time to whip the club back into shape."

I smile at her. "Good. Sir's been saying it's needed."

"Yes, it's overdue." She nods. "But we're on it now. Keep us in the loop."

"I will."

She leaves me to moon over the fine supplies. After some more slapping, groaning, and whispering, Emily rushes over. Bouncing curls, a ruffled black, turquoise, and pink dress, the heavy musk of sex, and a huge grin.

I wrap her in a hug. Without the platforms, I tower over her. With the platforms, at six feet five, I'm almost crushing her into my navel. "How are you, sweetheart?"

"Good. Daddy says hi. He's going to the gym for a few hours and then he's coming to get me for dinner. Can you and Master Bull join us?"

"How about you come to ours? Kiki's still recovering and we don't like to leave her alone for very long."

"That would be great!" Emily says with her usual enthusiasm. "Could I help cook?"

"Of course, sweetheart. Sir and Kiki will love a change from my microwaved dinners."

Giggling, she elbows me. "You don't."

Of course, I don't. Part of my service to our master is that I make at least one home-cooked meal a day. While doting on Kiki, I've been making three.

"Mmm, show me these books, sweetie, and let me get to work."

With a huge smile, she does.

a smacky tail

BLUNTS MEMBERS AND SUBMISSIVES - TWITCH

"TODAY, TWITCH!" Bull roars from the front hallway.

I meet the eyes of my partner in the large mirror she's sitting in front of as I finish curling her hair.

"So impatient." I roll my eyes.

Although we conspire in all things against our partner and Dom, we do it so he can't overhear. Bull's punishments are epic enough without catching our insubordination.

I finish the last corkscrew, wait a moment for it to cool so I'm not damaging the fiber, crunch it, then separate it into the pile of golden-brown curls sweeping over Kiki's shoulder. I blow an air-kiss across her forehead, not wanting to smudge my gloss, although this product promises that it's transfer-proof.

"You look stunning, darling," I tell her.

She smiles back at me. She is looking much better. A funny bump near her nipple turned into a lump that turned into a double-mastectomy. The doctors tell us they got it all before it metastasized and that the chemo was just a precaution, but between the surgery

128

and chemotherapy, my once-glowing partner was a wan shadow of herself for several months. Today, she has color in her cheeks that I didn't have to apply. If her eyes aren't yet as bright and lively as they were, that's okay because she's still with me. Still my Kinky Kiki. My partner in crime. My love. My life.

"Twitch, goddamn it, don't make me come up there!" My other love roars from downstairs.

"Doesn't he know perfection like this takes time?" I huff.

Kiki chuckles. "Now you're just stalling to piss him off."

I am, a little. Because sometimes it's good to thwart your Dom in low-key ways. It helps build up all that frustration that leads to explosive sex.

That's my theory anyway.

I grab the wrap I've picked to complement the dress Pence designed for Kiki. No one was more surprised than this man right here when that nasty brat showed up at the door with a box and a wary smile. Who knew there was a soul under all that evil? And evidently quite a talented designer.

Kiki's given the dress a trial run and had nothing but praise for it. It's lined with something that keeps her warm, which has been a serious problem since the surgery, but also feels light and good against her hyper-sensitive skin. I wanted to wrap her up in fleece and satin and other non-breathable fabrics, but all they did was make her sweat. I've had to become a reluctant investor in cotton—cotton!—and appreciate whatever magic's Pence has wrought that's keeping Kiki comfortable on this first outing since her surgery.

I drape the blue cotton shawl around her shoulders and step back to admire her. "Doesn't that bring out your eyes?"

"Yes, Twitch," she says in that way she does when she's both enabling me in pissing off our Dom and also running a little low on patience herself.

Not wanting to test that patience, because illness has taken a toll on Kiki's temper, I pick up my crown from the dresser, fasten it into my hair, and shrug into a black faux feathered jacket to match my skirt. We'll be among friends all day, so Bull gave me permission to be a little extra. I put the finishing touches on this black swan ensemble a few weeks before Kiki's diagnosis but haven't worn it. It feels right to unveil it on her first outing.

"Magnificent," Kiki says, grinning. She's the one who gave me my first crown and told me no matter what happened, I'd always be her queen. I've tried to live up to the title every day since.

Today's no exception.

"Off we go, then," I say, grabbing the handles of her wheelchair.

It's a nice day—surprisingly warm and sunny for so late in the fall—so we're walking the fifteen minutes to Blunts. Kiki's managing very well around the house now, but she still gets fatigued after a few minutes of walking, so a condition of Bull taking us to Blunts today was that she be in the wheelchair. She didn't put up any kind of fight, which told me everything I needed to know about her energy level. I staged a token resistance, but it was more against Bull trying to micro-manage every moment of Kiki's recovery than making sure the wheelchair was on hand all day. I love him, but Sir really is a control freak.

I wheel Kiki to the building's elevator, which we fortunately had before her illness. I didn't use it for much other than accessing the building's underground garage since I always need more cardio, but it has been a Goddessend.

Bull's waiting for us on the ground floor of our three-story. He's leaning against the door, arms crossed over his chest, legs crossed at the ankle. He smiles at Kiki when I push her chair out of the elevator but glowers at me.

"You look the same as you did an hour ago," he grumbles. "We're late."

I roll my eyes. Yes, I had on my puffed shirt, feathered skirt, and thigh-high boots an hour ago. But I hadn't started on my makeup and more importantly, Kiki's wig was more dirty-blonde labradoodle than golden-brown fabulousness and *something* had to be done about that, no matter how late it's made us.

"Queens are always exactly on time," I remind Sir.

Bull grumbles all the way out onto the street. Happily, the blue sky and mild breeze cheer him up quickly. He starts picking up colorful, fallen leaves and handing them to Kiki. She has a bouquet of them before we've gone six blocks. Bull's wearing his happy-puppy face. I love the man; I really do. Never more than when he's taking childlike delight in doting on our girl.

We go through security at Blunts and Dan-the-doorman comes to take Kiki's chair from me to wheel her through the handicapped entrance. I've known Dan for years. I trust Dan. I *absolutely fucking hate* him putting his hands on the chair and taking Kiki away from me. As I follow Bull up into the club, I'm shaking.

While we wait for Dan to bring Kiki through, Bull reaches under my feathered skirt and pinches my ass. "Fuck's wrong with you?"

"Nothing," I huff.

"Tweedle," he says, using the nickname he knows I hate to poke at me so I'll flare at him and spill what's wrong.

"We came this close to losing her." I pinch the air between my coffin nails. "I'm having trouble letting her out of my sight. That's all. I'll get over it."

I expect him to give me the Dom-look. Instead, he turns and folds me into his chest. "It's okay."

I let him hold me for a moment, until my lower lip gets away from me. Then I bat him off before saline does anything ridiculous like smudge my liner. "I know it is."

He releases me with a smile that tells me I'm not fooling him. His hand settles on my lower back and stays there even when Dan wheels Kiki through and turns over the chair to me. She's twirling her red, gold, and brown leaf bouquet and looking around with a smile. I check in with her anyway.

"Doing okay? Anything you want? Water? Potty?"

Bull snorts, probably at hearing me use the word "potty." I ignore him to focus on Kiki.

"No, I'm fine," Kiki tells me, her eyes straying beyond the handicap entrance vestibule into the club, where excited chatter fills the hallway.

"Okay, if you need anything, absolutely anything—"

"I'm good, hon. Come on, we're missing the fun."

"Ooo-kay. *Avante.*" I push her chair out into the hallway.

We walk (and roll) under a huge archway of paper flowers, hung with a banner that proclaims: "Blunts Bondage Marketplace." On either side of the long hallway that runs down the middle of the building, there are canvas booths, painted to look like wood. Each booth has its own little striped awning. The whole look is very 1862 Great London Exposition. I glance around, expecting one of the house subs to sweep by in a cage crinoline. A sign at the end of the hallway points down the stairwell to the "Den of Iniquity," aka, the nightclub. There will be dancing down there later, I have no doubt, but I want Kiki home and tucked up in bed looong before then.

Bull lifts his eyebrows. "This is new."

He's been a Master at Blunts for longer than Kiki or I have known him, well over a decade, so he would know. I haven't always been the biggest fan of his membership. After he collared me, I thought he'd quit. What does he want with hamburger when he's got filet mignon at home? But seeing how forlorn Bull was after his friend Logan pulled back from the club, I began to realize the club isn't just about kinky play for Sir. It's about friendship, community, and a sense of belonging.

Bull gets along really well with the other Masters and Mistresses; he counts them among his closest friends. He's on the management committee of the club and has been for years. He's respected and valued. All the adoration Kiki and I give him doesn't replace the esteem of his peers.

One of those peers walks out from under the archway and greets Bull with a warm handshake. The Masters, Mistresses, and house submissives of Blunts come in all sizes, shapes, and colors, which is something I've always liked about Sir's club. But the Master greeting Bull got a double-blessing from the Goddess in the looks department. Tall, athletic, strong features, and a mop of dark brown waves that anyone, man or woman, would want to run their fingers through, Master Rob has it on the outside. I've always thought the package over-compensated for the contents, if you know what I mean. Nothing against Master Rob, of course. It's just that there didn't seem to be a lot of substance beneath the surface.

But after a disastrous run with one of the house masochists, Rob's started scening regularly with Shannie. And I got that tea from the leaf, not just the subbie vine. Shannie's one of the most honest, hardest-working people I've met, so if she sees something in Rob beyond his killer hair, there must be more to the contents of his package than I'd noticed before.

Rob says a quick hello to me and then fawns over Kiki. That's the point of today. The whole bondage marketplace thing is fun, but there's nothing here Bull hasn't bought, or made when it comes down to it, since Bull's quite handy. We're here because it gets Kiki out of the house and into an environment where she's comfortable and well-liked.

One of the architects of this environment saunters over from a booth where he's offering to "Smack a Bottom for a Cause." Javier's shed the jacket of his classic Dior twill suit and rolled up the sleeves of his custom-tailored black shirt, showing off forearms kept toned by hours of bottom-smacking. He shakes hands with Bull and me, then shoo-es Rob out of the way so he can bend over and hug Kiki. When he straightens, he grins at me, showing teeth as shiny as his pate, and far too white for the smoker he is.

"You will be volunteering that bottom, won't you, my dear?" he asks, although it's more of a command than a question.

"I mean, I *would* but—"

"Yes, you will," Bull says. "And I think I might sweeten the pot. One smack from every Master or Mistress here today and I'll double what you've collected today, J."

"That's very generous," Javier says approvingly.

I level Bull with a glare that promises so much more than murder.

He smiles at me. "It'll get your mind off things. And I'll give you a get out of jail free card, which you know I rarely do."

That's true. Bull's a strict Dom, which I usually like, but am not feeling today.

"If you can find someone who hasn't had their ass paddled already and convince them to take half your hits, they can and I'll still double the pot."

"I know what you're doing," I tell him.

"I know you do. You're going to let me do it, too. You need it."

I toss my head at him. He's not right. Well, he might be a little right. *Of course* I'm worried about Kiki. *Of course* the last several months have been stressful. But I'm managing just fine, thank you very much. I even started a new job in the club library so I'm not in the house fussing over Kiki twenty-four-seven. The only thing a hundred hits—because *that's* how many Masters and Mistresses there are—will do is exfoliate my ass. Which is unnecessary since I just did a sea-salt body scrub yesterday. It won't be any kind of stress relief.

"Quick spin around the block to see if there's anything you want as a reward for taking a hundred for the team and then you can get down to it," Bull tells me, his grin straight out of a latte-with-dairy-fueled nightmare.

I scowl at him.

"Twitch!"

My staring contest with my Dom is interrupted by the arrival of a Victorian fairy. With wings. She barrels into my arms without regard for either my costume or hers. A few black feathers probably transfer over, but they'll just enhance her get-up.

Once I finish hugs and air-kisses, I hold her at arm's length. "Spectacular. Astounding. Breathtaking. Phenomenal. Marvelous. *Inconceivable.*"

Emily preens under each word, twisting from side to side so I can take in the full glory of her costume. A velvet top-hat with a black veil perches atop her glossy curls. Mechanical moth wings rise from the shoulders of an emerald-green walking dress with leather belts and ruffles, gathered and ruched in the front to expose her slender legs in fishnet stockings and knee-high leather boots. Brass goggles bristling with knobs and colored lenses are perched on the brim of her hat and a chain made of gears defines her little waist. She is a steampunk fairy vision.

On the last word she leans in. "I do not think it means what you think it means."

I give her a huge wink. "As you wish."

She links her arm through mine. "Come see, come see."

"Come buy, come buy, apples and quinces, lemons and oranges, plump unpeck'd cherries, melons and raspberries, bloom-down-cheek'd peaches, swart-headed mulberries," I say, reciting a poem by Christina Rossetti. I found a damaged first edition of her poetry in Blunts' library a few days ago. Emily and I spent a happy afternoon reading together while I fixed the binding and gilded the cover and spine, because *first edition.*

"All ripe together, in summer weather—Morns that pass by, fair eves that fly; Come buy, come buy," Emily joins in. "Next year I'll make it a goblin market."

I chuckle. "That seems fitting for this crowd."

She elbows me. "You're terrible."

"Mmm-hmm, the Terrible Twitch."

She drags me over to a booth selling irritants for chemical play. Jars of peppermint and wintergreen. Tall glass vials of cinnamon and pepper oils. Pots of arthritis rub, Tiger Balm, Icy-Hot, and several other mineral rubs. Emily's daddy, Master Logan, is manning the booth and he leans over his wares with an evil leer.

"New clientele," he says, rubbing his gray-gloved hands together. He's wearing a suit in a shiny blue fabric with a brown velvet smoking jacket and top hat. Half-moon spectacles with blue lenses perch on the end of his nose over the most ridiculous, curled walrus mustache I've ever seen. The mustache waggles side to side as he talks. "Come to sample Doctor Logan's world-famous snake oil lubricant?"

"Yes, Daddy!" Emily chirps.

He picks up a brown bottle and holds it out with a flourish. "It stimulates. It chills. It heats. It provides relief. Good for man and beast!"

Emily begins giggling. "It can't do all those things at the same time, Daddy."

"Oh, my sweet, naïve, little lady, it can do all those things and more. It expands. It contracts. It causes the wanted parts to swell and the unwanted parts to shrink! It relieves pain. It itches; it tingles. It stimulates hair growth in the right places and depilates the wrong ones. It is Doctor Logan's perfect liniment. Yours for only one silver dollar."

"I have one here!" Emily fishes around in a small purse hanging from her belt and waves what looks like a silver poker chip.

"No, no," Bull's deep voice comes from behind us. "Put your money away, Emmy. I'll pay this snake oil salesman."

Logan claps a hand to his chest. "You wound me, good sir."

Bull wheels Kiki up to the booth and Logan hands her the bottle with a flourish. Bull passes Logan a silver poker chip.

Logan holds out his hand. "Ahem."

"You said it was a silver dollar," Bull protests.

"For the little lady. For foul skeptics and doubting Thomases such as yourself, sir, it's a fiver."

Bull chuckles but he counts out four more silver chips and slaps them in Logan's glove. "Shyster."

Logan grins at him and pockets the chips. "Skeptic. You three sticking around for dinner and dancing afterward?"

I start to shake my head but Kiki cranes her neck to look back at both of us. The naked hope on her face shreds my refusal.

"We'll see how Kiki feels after a couple of hours," I hedge.

"We'll keep seats at our table for you," Logan offers. "Now, be sure to leave Doctor Logan's Snake Oil lubricant a good review! Satisfied customers are all any good salesman desires."

Giggling, Emily runs around the edge of the booth for a kiss, and a grope, before she returns to my side and drags me onward. The next booth has a spread of . . . things posed on a crimson velvet cloth.

I have nearly a decade of experience in the lifestyle. And I'm not completely sure what some of the *things* are.

I pick up a luminous animal skull with a twisted, multicolored, tentacle tongue stretching out from the jaws. The tongue flops in my hand, surprisingly heavy and solid.

I lift my eyes to the grinning submissive behind the booth.

"The demon Abraxas," Fleur says. "Very popular among those who like a deeper *prod*."

Emily bursts into giggles.

I do like a deeper prod. Who doesn't? But I'm not sure I want it from the rainbow tentacle tongue. Besides, Bull's . . . tentacle . . . is ten and three-quarters inches. Yes, we've measured. And that's a wicked deep prod, let me tell you. It took him months to train my ass to take it.

I put the skull down and pick up the next thing. It's a mechanical hand, with wires and clockwork buried inside the transparent skin. The splayed fingers are oddly long and thick and when I look more closely I realize they're—

"Edward Dickenhands," Fleur says. "Satisfy up to five at once. Rack 'em, stack 'em, and pack 'em."

Emily's bent over, she's giggling so hard. "Fleur's started a line of silicone sex toys."

"You look so innocent, darling," I say to her. "When did this happen?"

Fleur shrugs, her pale shoulder rising out of the off-the-shoulder gown she's wearing. Her costume is Victorian milk-maid as interpreted by a medieval tavern wench, with lots of tattered lace and black satin ribbons holding together a minimum of gauzy cloth. It's a very a-historical ensemble, but she rocks it.

"I needed PT on my ankle," she tells me. "I had some downtime, so I thought I'd see what I could do with all the stage makeup I've learned over the years. Turns out there are a lot of perverts out there looking for the strange and unusual."

I knew she'd sprained her ankle. She told everyone it was an accident, but I've met her not-quite-Ex and figure he had more to do with it than the stairs she said she slipped on. I thought the sprain kept her from dancing for a week or two. It sounds worse than that.

"You and I need a catch up, girlfriend," I tell her.

"Love to," she says. "I just didn't want to bother you when you were focused on Kiki."

I glance over my shoulder at Bull and Kiki, who have rolled to another booth and are talking to Maude, who is dressed up like a medusa, her hair wired into a crown of snakes and sprayed iridescent green. Well, a medusa in a Victorian day dress. This really is the bazaar of the bizarre.

"Thank you, sweetie, but I think she's really doing much better."
Fleur smiles. "Lunch Friday?"
"It's a date. I'll text you."

I lean over the menagerie of terrifying implements to give her a hug and kiss before following my little guide to the next booth and the next. We make a slow circuit of the marketplace, laughing together over the crazier items on display.

When we get back to the flower arch, we find Bull and Kiki at Fleur's booth. Bull's holding the Edward Dickenhands, twisting it so the dick-fingers wave at Kiki, to her laughing delight.

I roll my eyes at both the implement and his antics.

"Oh, yeah," he says. "How much, Fleur?"

Bull doesn't blink at the price she names, just nods and signs the club chit when she holds it out. I don't object, although I'm going to hide that thing as soon as we get home. I enjoy a little grotesquerie as much as the next man, but all those waving finger-cocks? Gruesome. It's as bad as the Stormtrooper butt plug Bull brought back after a visit to one of his crazy college friends in San Francisco. There are many things I'm perfectly happy for Bull to put up my ass, but a Stormtrooper is not one of them. Besides, Stormtroopers have terrible aim. With my luck, I'd end up with it sticking out of my ear.

Kiki looks thrilled when Bull drops the wrapped-up Edward Dickenhands into her lap. She picks it up and shakes it so the finger-dicks inside the tissue paper wriggle wildly.

I roll my eyes.

It is, of course, Master Javier who catches me in the act.

He slides his arm through mine. "My dear," he says, his accent both New York and boarding school. "Anyone would think you're avoiding me."

I peck his cheek. That's allowed under Sir's rules. "Anyone would be right."

He chuckles. "I think that's an extra swat. Come along. Let's get started. There's a queue."

He's right, damn the man. Five Doms are lingering around the spanking booth, clearly waiting for my bottom to become available. "Bu-but—"

"Yes, your butt is in demand," Javier says wryly.

I elbow him even as I let him pull me toward the booth. "Anyone would think you're a sadist."

Javier's husky, smoker's laugh breaks out. "Anyone would be right."

As we walk around behind the booth's canvas front, the true horror of what Bull's committed me to dawns. There's a wooden spanking bench so old the wood is black. Will that even hold me? I don't think it will hold me. And what about splinters?

"Darling, that has to be a health and safety violation."

Javier snorts. "That's the problem with your generation. No respect for tradition."

"I have a great deal of respect for tradition," I object. "Just no respect for implements that should have been consigned to an antique dealer a decade ago."

"Get your pretty ass over it," Javier says.

At least he appreciates my fine ass.

I bend down to the bench and get my knees on the lower "seat." The upper "seat" is much too low for me. I'm going to have to fold in half. My poor back. I could tell from a distance this thing would be the death of me.

Before I accordion myself, Javier reaches down and cranks something. The upper seat rises to a comfortable height for me to rest my chest on.

I can be a petty betty from time to time, but I haven't lost my manners. "Thank you, Master Javier."

His eyes search my face for sarcasm and when he doesn't find it, he smiles. "You're very welcome, my dear. On you go. I want first swat."

I restrain an eyeroll, which would get me more than a swat.

As I settle onto the curved, upper seat, my hands land naturally on rounded grips which frame the seat. Despite its antiquity and lack of padding, the spanking bench is comfortable. There are grooves either carved or worn into it for my shins. The upper seat is tilted as well as raised, so my head's not lower than my ass. Bull is not really a spanker—that's more of Kiki's thing when she switches—but on the rare occasions when he spanks me, he favors over-the-knee, a position which compounds the misery of the spanking with pressure in the sinuses. My sniffles last longer than the sting of the spanking. I appreciate that I'll have my head up for this little exercise.

Bull's booming voice sounds over the murmurs of the waiting Doms. "I think someone might benefit from a little restraint."

I glance up at my Sir. He winks at me. He doesn't restrain me during impact play; controlling my response to pain is part of the submission he demands from me. By telling Javier to restrain me, he's releasing me from that requirement. That earns him a wink and a smile.

There's no shortage of willing hands to strap me into the chair. I appreciate Master Rob's perfectly tousled locks a great deal less when they're bent over my arm as he buckles down my wrist.

Once I'm strapped to the creaking antique, Javier lifts my feathered skirt and pins it out of the way. I'd never criticize my Sir, but I wish he'd develop Master Javier's appreciation for couture. Cool air kisses my ass above the tops of my thigh-high boots and I'm glad I've worn a garter thong so the crowd has something more than a boring old black string to stare at.

Master Javier runs his fingers under the garter straps, creating a clear "target." Then he pats my bare ass.

"Franci Christian?" he asks. "I like the brand myself."

Thinking of the supremely dominant Javier wearing a mesh garter thong keeps a smile on my face as he begins a rapid tapping to warm up my skin and muscle. I focus on my hands gripping the spanking bench to get past the initial sting. It will take a while before it feels good; I just have to endure until it does.

Javier's hard hand crashing down makes me twitch and shiver. A second crash has me blinking back wetness. Goddess wept, his hand is like granite.

He rubs the sting in, pressing hard with the flat of his hands, soothing all those angry, angry nerve endings. Another thing Master Javier does exceptionally well. By the time Javier steps away and Master Rob takes his place, the spot on my ass-cheek where he hit me is burning like I lay on the beach without sunscreen—something I'd never, ever do, of course—but it no longer feels like he's made me sit on hot coals.

Master Rob's palm on my unmarked cheek makes a dull pop. It leaves behind a square of warmth, but barely any sting. Unremarkable, like his personality.

Master Nico is next and he makes me pay for every time I've smarted off in his presence. He slaps the same spot Javier hit. The reverberation of it runs all the way up my spine. He doesn't rub it in, but flicks his fingers between my legs to tap my balls. My eyes cross and my whole body judders.

Nico walks away chuckling.

The long train of Mistress Dana's saloon-style dress rustles as she takes Nico's place. She starts by pressing both palms into my ass-cheeks, working into the muscle. Her strong fingers roll my skin up and then back. By the time she delivers a sharp tap to each cheek and then circles her palms over the spots she's hit, the burn of impact has spread into a low-key, suffused warmth.

Just like my Kiki, who does fore- and aftercare so very right.

Or used to.

Master Jay steps up. Followed by Master Martin who has hands like marshmallows. Then Mistress Maude in her snake-tressed glory. She rubs in the sting like the pro she is, too. I swallow a small moan as her hands press and knead. Sir would not like me whimpering for another Dom.

The next few hands have things to prove. Master Drew, who I barely know, winds up and smacks like he's trying to hit a home run. Chairman Chess has a hand as hard as Javier's and it must be the size of a dinner-plate because he manages to catch both cheeks with one slap. Master Franco, who is an asshole on a good day, lets me know he's *not* having a good day when he lays into my sit-spots and makes me yelp.

I get a break with some of the fluffier Doms: Jimmy, Hart, and Ty. Then Master Ten steps up.

I tense. I can't help it. Bull's never had much good to say about Ten. After something happened with DirtyGurl, Bull's had a number of closed-door conversations with the other members of the management committee. I wouldn't listen at a closed door, of course, but if I just *happened* to overhear something . . . I mean, how else do you get the tea?

And there is serious tea. Bull's used the words suspension and probation during those hush-hush convos.

I have no doubt my ass is about to pay for all that antagonism.

A sharp noise brings my head up. And up. To meet Bull's eyes as he takes a wide-legged stance near my head. He finishes clearing his throat, nods at me, raises his gaze, and crosses his arms over his wide chest.

"Problem?" Ten asks in his deep grumble from behind me.

"Not if you don't make one," Bull says.

"Are you accusing me of something?" Ten asks.

"Not yet," Bull responds.

A tiny creaking noise breaks the heavy silence that follows. I swear it's my muscles tightening and creaking like ship ropes and not this stupid splinter I'm strapped to.

Maude breaks the stand-off, sweeping in with a swirl of green silk. "Gentlemen. Let's all behave that way."

"I'm not the one making a scene," Ten says.

"You're the cause of every scene," Bull retorts. "I won't have you taking out your issues on my submissive."

"That's what you think of me?" Ten's voice drops an octave. "That I'd hurt a submissive to jab at you?"

"I think your self-control's worse than a week-old puppy's and you strike at the nearest target when you're pissed off. I won't let my submissive be that target."

With a harsh scrape of his bootheel against the parquet floor, Ten turns and walks off.

"Bull," Maude says softly. "Was that necessary?"

Sir chuffs. "You may believe his bullshit excuses, but I don't. He needs counseling. If we're not going to force him to get it, at least I can protect my submissive from him."

Maude sighs. "This isn't the time or place to discuss this."

"Agreed," Bull says. "Whenever anyone wants to talk, I'm ready. But there's going to be a vote, Maude, and soon."

With a rustle of serpents, Maude shakes her head. "Let's speak tomorrow." She pats my back. "Your submissive's been very patient. Let's not keep him waiting. Shedo, are you next?"

Bull nods and steps back.

Master Shedo gives me a precise, sharp smack that makes my ass tingle. He presses it in with a firm palm before giving way to Master Karl, who I should probably fear because he's just as much of a sadist as Master Ten. But Karl is never predictable. He scratches my reddened cheeks with his blunt nails, igniting my nerves, before barely tapping my ass. Between the stimulation of my smarting skin and the placement of the tap, a shiver runs straight up my spine.

"Thank you, Master Karl," I say. "Your evil is unmatched."

He walks off chuckling.

The Doms keep coming. Word has clearly gotten around. I lose track of who has and hasn't had a turn somewhere in the forties, knowing I still have too many to go. Despite the many who have rubbed the sting in, my ass is on fire. Each whisper of air across my outraged skin makes me flinch. A dull, digging ache has worked through my muscle and is boring into my bones.

Bull took Kiki on another stroll around the marketplace—and returned with something that looks more like a medieval mace than a butt plug—while I was wincing my way through the thirties. When he returned, he fetched up against the neighboring stall and has been chatting with Master Javier.

I know they're keeping their eyes on me. I know neither of them will let it get to the point where I'm injured. The pain isn't as bad as the times Bull has whipped me, but it's slower, more enduring. It *demands* more of me.

With all our focus on Kiki's illness and recovery, I've had very little asked of me lately. I feel it when for the first time in a very long time, I consider calling yellow.

Then I give myself a firm mental lecture. I'm *hurting*. I'm not hurt. Pain is passing. Submission is enduring. I am more than my body. I am will. I am strength. I am beauty. Those things have nothing to do with a reddened ass. My Sir wanted me to do this. His will is supreme.

Settled in my own head, I tense all my muscles, then force them to relax group by group, starting with my head and working down to my toes.

Bull notices I'm doing relaxation exercises and comes over to lay his hand between my shoulder blades.

"Good boy," he says quietly. "Tense and relax two more times for me."

"Yes, Sir."

By the third cycle of tensing and relaxing, everything's soft and giving again, even my burning butt. I settle comfortably onto the chair and tip my ass up for the next hit.

It's Emily's daddy, Master Logan. He takes a moment to straighten my crown before he gives me a sharp but not brutal spank.

Emily steps up with a flutter of her wings. She's not thinking about taking a shot at my ass, is she? I *will* retaliate. There's only so much even a Queen can be expected to take.

But no, Emily drags a reticent figure with her and when she reaches me, pushes him forward.

Neither the Harlequin costume nor his black and white face paint is enough to conceal Pence's lean body and sharp-featured face. If he takes a shot at my ass, I'll do more than retaliate.

When he just stands there, shifting from foot to foot with a faint jingle of the bells on his shoes and tips of his hat, Emily nudges him.

"Go on," she urges.

I look from him to her and back to him.

"Twitch, ask him."

My mind is utterly blank of anything I'd want to ask Pence. "Uh, thanks again for Kiki's dress. Any chance you could make her another one?"

Emily blows out a breath. "Omi-goodness! Ask him if he'll take the rest of the spanks for you."

Oh. I eye Pence. He's looking anywhere but at me. The ceiling seems to hold particular fascination.

"Pence, would you be a dear and take the rest of the spanks?"

Pence nods.

I'm honestly shocked. I assumed the dress was a one-off, and that Master Harold asked him to make it after Bull mentioned Kiki's first outing. Is Pence trying . . . to be friends?

"Well, okay," I say. "Thank you, Pence."

I begin pushing up from the chair, expecting Pence and Emily to help with the straps.

"Wait a minute," says a sweet, familiar voice. Kiki rises from her wheelchair and walks past Emily and Pence. "I want a turn."

"Kiki? You're not too tired?"

She bends over and grabs a handful of my hair. As she gives it a firm pull, she whispers in my ear, "That's beloved, benevolent Mistress when I'm about to spank you, isn't it? And no, I'm not too tired. Because the two men who mean the most to me in the whole world have taken such good care of me. Lie back down and remember who you belong to."

I slump back onto the chair. "Yes, beloved, benevolent Mistress."

She tugs my hair again, lighting up all the nerves in my scalp and sending a hard shiver through me, before she releases it and shuffles around behind me. She rubs her cool palms over my aching, burning ass.

Then she gives me two sharp slaps, flexing her palm to maximize the sting. I gulp and breathe hard through the burn. She lets it smart for a long moment before she starts to rub.

"Thank you, beloved, benevolent Mistress."

With a last pat, she puts the straps of my garters back in place, takes the pins out of my skirt and smooths it down. She gets to work on the leg restraints while Pence and Emily unbuckle my arms.

Bull's there to help me off the chair when the last of the restraints is undone. Pence climbs into my place. Master Harold's the first one up and he doesn't waste a moment lighting up his boy's ass.

Wincing at my fiery backside, I follow Bull back toward Kiki's chair. Kiki lingers near the spanking chair for a minute, chatting with Logan and Emily, before she joins us. When I start to fuss about getting her back in her chair, she holds up an imperious hand.

"Where do you belong?" she asks me.

I gape at her. She hasn't asked me that in months. "At your feet?" My voice is a squeak.

"At your feet . . . what?"

I fold to the floor with as much grace as I can, and caress her ankles. "At your feet, my beloved, benevolent Mistress."

"That's right," she says. "Good boy."

She steps into her chair and settles herself, as regally as any monarch.

"I'm tired," she says airily. "You may take me home now."

I kiss her feet before I rise and take the handles of her wheelchair. Bull straightens my crown with a smile.

We set off, the three of us, toward home. Kiki has that horrible Dickenhands toy in her lap and I have no doubt that, after a nap, she'll want to do something terrible to me with it.

I look forward to it, because my Kiki is back.

The members and house submissives of Blunts will return in Daddy P.I. 3.0.

about the author

Reader, bunny-wrangler, fire-spinner, and writer of things. I like my science hard and my romance harder.

Constitutionally incapable of settling into a genre, I bounce in and out of contemporary mystery, space opera, and paranormal romance, all with a decidedly kinky twist.

Sign up to my newsletter for a free book, sneak peeks, and updates:

https://dl.bookfunnel.com/r94ra9ilza

Need more Blunts Tales? Get early access and exclusive stories in my Patreon: https://www.patreon.com/ejfrost

Bring cake.

If you've enjoyed *Blunts Tales*, please consider leaving a review on your platform of choice. Reviews mean everything to independent authors!

The Daddy P.I. Casefiles

Kinky Mystery Romance.

Death.

Pirates.

A stalker.

A missing collar.

And, always, a Daddy-Dom to the rescue!

Join P.I. James Logan and his little, Emily Martin, on the investigations of their lives in these three collected books. Start with their first meeting at the Salt City kink expo; explore an exclusive New York City club on their first date; ride the wild waves of the Mexican Sunset cruise as they seek the source of a drug that's killing passengers; return with them to New York as they track down a vicious stalker; and end with their collaring ceremony in a haunted inn in picturesque Niagara Falls.

This box set contains Book 0.5 (previously unavailable on paid platforms), Book 1.0, Book 2.0, and a bonus novella, The Case of the Missing Collar.

Read the box set here, free to read with a Kindle Unlimited subscription:
https://books2read.com/u/31YOYa

Neon Blue

M/F, Paranormal Romance Series.

Demons.

Can't live with 'em.

Can't kill 'em.

My name is Tsara Elizabeth Faa, and I have a demon problem.

A very serious demon problem. My ex-best friend has summoned an incubus and left me to deal with him. Now he's after my soul.

Thing is, the more time I spend with him, the more I want to give it to him.

Read *Neon Blue* here, free to read with a Kindle Unlimited subscription:
https://books2read.com/u/mZZ292

Capricorn

M/F, Paranormal Romance.

Evan Lords is a Capricorn, but that's meant nothing to him for nearly forty years. Less than nothing during the seven years he's spent in prison for a murder he didn't commit.

Now, the Helm of the Sea Goat has called Evan's name and the Capricorns have arranged his release so their promised leader can save them from mysterious force Hell-bent on destroying their sacred charge: wild magic.

But his freedom isn't the only thing Evan lost seven years ago. He also left behind his love, his little. With the fate of the world's magic hanging in the balance can Evan save the Capricorn Guild, and will it cost him the woman he loves?

Read Capricorn here, free to read with a Kindle Unlimited subscription: https://books2read.com/u/bQjx5D

Capricorn is a stand-alone story within the *Masters of the Zodiac* series. Characters cross over from the author's *Bad Boys of Bevington* series. *Capricorn* is intended for mature readers only.

Snowburn

M/F , Scifi Romance.

Unleash the monster. Save the girl.

Hale Hauser is a Company killer. Perfectly engineered, highly trained, superbly effective. But when ordered to assassinate his own kind, Hale rebels, and the Company buries him in a hole so deep that no one has ever escaped.

After escaping, Hale hides on Kuseros, a backwater Colony on the Deep Frontier. He begins a new life as Sandringham Snow, pilot and smuggler. Hired by Kez, a local runner, to retrieve a box of black-market glands, Hale follows her through the maze of strange loyalties and twisted customs of Kuseros' underground gangs. In payment, he takes the one thing only a woman can give him, and discovers the one thing his new life is missing.

But Kez has a secret, which will threaten them both. To protect her, Hale must unleash the monster. Can he control the killer inside long enough to discover the truth before it destroys them? Or will he lose everything just as he's found it?

Read *Snowburn* here, free to read with a Kindle Unlimited subscription: **https://books2read.com/u/m2Z9ko.**

www.ingramcontent.com/pod-product-compliance
Lightning Source LLC
Chambersburg PA
CBHW070901160726
48004CB00003B/1199